Her So Called Husband

by

Chenell Parker

Text ChenellParker
to 22828 to be
added to my emailing list

Join my reader's group Chenell's Chatty Corner *on FaceBook*

TO BOSTON, WITH LOVE

WHEN IT COMES BACK AROUND

YOU'RE THE BEST PART

FEELING BLEU

Tyree

Chapter 1

I sat around my darkened living room drinking from the bottle of Cîroc that was cradled in my hands. For the past week, drinking was all that I seemed to do. That was the only thing that took away the pain that I was feeling at the moment.

Even after I walked in on Alexus naked in bed with her ex, I was still having a hard time coming to terms with it all. Hurt was not even the right word to describe how I was feeling. I was devastated. I lost count of the many times I asked her if she was done with him and, each time, she looked me right in my eyes and swore that she was. She was always saying how happy she was with me but, obviously, she wasn't happy enough.

I hated myself for stepping outside of my character when it came to Alexus. Never being one to involve others in my business, enlisting the help of Keanna to find out the truth was something that I should have never had to do. All I ever asked for was honesty and she couldn't even give me that. So, in return, I turned into the same thing that Alexus had become: a liar.

The whole story about me going to Texas for business was a lie. I just had to see for myself what went on with her when I wasn't around. Even after Keanna told me about seeing Alexus with her cousin, Dre, I still had some reservations. I loved her so much that I was willing to turn a blind eye to the truth. It wasn't until after I talked to her brother that my eyes were wide open. She had me under the impression that she was staying with her brother at one point when we had a falling out. But according to him, he hadn't seen her in over two months.

It was only then that I came up with the business meeting in Texas lie. I damn near begged her to stay at my house, but she kept refusing and now I know why. I would have called the whole charade off if she agreed to stay at my house, instead of Jada's. A part of me was happy that she didn't stay or I wouldn't have ever found out the truth about the games that she was playing. I sat there and replayed the events from last week in my head and got heated all over again.

When I got the call from Keanna telling me to meet her at Jada's house, I was hoping that nothing would come of it. Even after I got there, I didn't see the car that she told me her cousin would be driving. I saw Jada and Lex's car in the driveway, but that was all. Keanna's car was parked a few houses down, but that was to be expected since I was meeting her there.

I walked up the steps that led to my cousin's front door with legs that felt like they weighed one hundred pounds each. Yelling could be heard coming from upstairs, even before I made it into the house. I was taking my time at first, but that quickly changed when I walked through the front door. I took the steps two at a time with my heart beating just as fast with every step I took. Jada's was the first set of eyes to meet mine as I walked down the hall that led to her spare bedroom. Her eyes silently pleaded for me to leave as the tears cascaded down her face rapidly. I knew then that whatever I was about to see was anything but good.

"Just listen for a minute," I remembered Jada saying through her tears.

She had her hand on my chest, trying to stop me from entering the room. I pushed her hand down and continued my walk. I stopped before I got to the room, preparing myself for what I was about to see next. Jada walked into the room and apologized to Alexus for what she knew was about to be the end of our relationship. Once she was done talking, I walked the rest of the way until I was standing directly in the doorway.

When Alexus saw me, all the color drained from her face as she dropped her head in shame. I looked over at her ex and the look of satisfaction on his face could not be missed. I didn't have to ask what was going on. Their naked bodies were enough evidence, even though they tried to shield it with the cover.

"That's what's up. At least I don't have to ask you no more. I got my answer. You can have that hoe," I said, talking to Dre while shaking my head at Alexus. The smirk on his face let me know that she was exactly what he wanted.

"Tyree, wait!" Alexus yelled to my departing back.

I walked down the stairs and didn't stop until I made it outside to my car. Jada was right behind me, trying to talk on behalf of her friend.

"Ty, I swear, we didn't know that he was coming over here. He just popped up and told us to open the door," she said as she followed me.

"You can miss me with all that bullshit. You're just as guilty as she is. We're cousins and you got her and this nigga laying up like they're paying rent up in this bitch or something."

"It's not even like that. She told him that she didn't want him anymore. She stopped answering the phone and everything. He just doesn't want to take no for an answer."

9

"It don't seem like she was trying to say no to me. Fucking a nigga is a hell of a way to say goodbye. So again, you and your girl can miss me with the bullshit."

I looked up and saw Keanna and Lex's sister coming out of the house. I knew why Keanna was here, but I was lost as to why she was here with Ayanna. I had a lot of unanswered questions, but I wasn't sure who to get a truthful answer from. I hopped in my car and peeled away, leaving Jada standing on the curb. As soon as I turned the corner, I spotted the car that Keanna told me belonged to her cousin, a CLS 500 with a personalized license plate that read "D-Mack". They were slick but, obviously, they weren't slick enough.

A few minutes later, I was shaken from my thoughts by the ringing of my doorbell. I knew who it was, even before I got up to look through the peephole. My sisters had been blowing my phone up for the past few hours. They were asking me if they could come and get Alexus' things that she left at my house. Today wasn't going to be any different than any other day. My answer was still no. If she wanted her shit, she would have to be woman enough to come and get it herself. She was going to face me, whether she wanted to or not. She tried calling too but she went unanswered, just like everyone else. This was one time that I refused to allow her to run from her problems.

"What do y'all want?" I asked my sisters once I opened the door. They walked pass me like I gave them an invitation to come in.

"Why is it so dark in here?" Trina asked, flipping on the light switch. I'd been sitting in the dark for so long that the light made me flinch and cover my eyes.

"Don't come in here touching my shit!" I yelled, hitting the wall switch to turn the lights off.

"You need to get up and get your ass up out of here. You smell bad and so does this house," Trina said, turning her nose up at me.

"Don't worry about me. What do y'all want?" I asked for the second time.

"You need to let us bring that girl her stuff. Her books are here and she has classes to go to," my sister, Tina, spoke up.

"I never stopped her from coming to get her stuff. I said that I'm not giving it to y'all, but she can come get it whenever she's ready." I took a drink from my almost empty bottle.

"I can't believe that you're acting like this. The drinking and the attitude are not you at all," Tina said.

"You can't believe that I'm acting like this?" I yelled, pointing to myself. "Y'all are acting like I did something wrong. I didn't get caught butt ass naked in the bed with my ex, so don't try to come at me with that guilt trip shit. I don't have anything to feel guilty about. I'm the one who's walking around with a broken heart while she's probably still off somewhere fucking a married man."

"No, she's not. She's been staying with Jada. We've been over there every day and he hasn't been over there once," Tina replied.

"I really don't give a fuck. If he wants her, he can have her."

I loved my sisters, but they were pissing me off right about now. They were standing here defending Alexus like she was a saint or something.

"That's messed up," Trina said, shaking her head.

I felt my anger rising, so I decided to end their visit before things got out of hand.

"Y'all need to go. Tell y'all friend that she know where her shit is at if she wants it." I opened my front door for them to leave.

Usually, I would go back on my word and cave in to their demands, but it wasn't happening this time. Alexus was going to face me one way or the other. They walked past me without saying anything else. I knew they were mad, but so was I. The only difference was, I was the only one who had a reason to be upset.

Chapter 2

I t'd been a little over a week since all the drama
unfolded with Lex and Tyree. I laughed every time
I thought about the look on her face when she saw
Tyree standing there while she was still naked in bed with Dre.
That was definitely a Kodak moment. There was no way in hell
that she could have lied her way out of that. I tried calling to
check on Tyree, but he never answered the phone. I guess he
was still going through the motions right now. I just hoped that
all my hard work wasn't in vain.

Honestly, I knew that I really didn't have a chance with
Tyree, but I was happy just as long as that bitch didn't have
him. Dre was still the same selfish bastard he'd always been.
He was pissed with me because Alexus didn't want to have
anything to do with him but that wasn't my problem. When he
agreed to help us set things up, he took that risk all on his own.

The original plan was for him to get her to come to his
house, but the plans changed at the last minute because she

refused to go. He ended up going to see her at Jada's house and that was even better. At first, I thought he changed his mind about everything, but he came through just like he said he would. He sent me a text letting me know that he was there, but I didn't go until he gave me the green light.

Ayanna still had a key to Jada's house, so things worked out better than we expected. I guess Dre thought that Lex would run to him since her and Tyree had broken up, but she did the opposite. She cut him off, just like Tyree cut her off. According to her sister, she hadn't been home since everything went down, so she was probably crashing at Jada's house.

On the other hand, life was pretty good for me right now and it seemed to be getting better. Working nights at the club was proving to be one of the best decisions that I'd ever made. I was making anywhere from two to three hundred a night, including tips. That might not have seemed like much to some but it was more than enough for me.

Most of my money came from the private dances that Ayanna and I did for some of the regulars. We did some wild shit in those private rooms and the customers ate it up. Ayanna and I were very attracted to each other so that helped a lot when we performed together.

Then, to my surprise, I got a call from Troy two days ago, telling me that he was being released tonight at midnight. I had been running around all day trying to make sure that everything was perfect for his first night home. I cooked enough food to feed an army and the house was spotless. I'd already taken off from the club for the next three days so that we could spend some much-needed time together. It would put a small dent in my bank account, but I could always make up for it.

I was still seeing Malik from time to time, but not as much as I use to. He was finally working again and, with me working at the club, it was hard for us to hook up. He had an attitude when I told him about Troy coming home. I didn't know if he was mad about us not being together as much, or if it was because he knew that his well had run dry. Even though he had a job, I still helped him out financially from time to time. On top of losing his car, he ended up getting evicted from his apartment as well. He was now living with his sister and her husband, and he was not very happy about it.

It was after ten when I pulled up to my apartment. I had just enough time to take a shower and prepare our room before it was time for me to go pick up Troy. I went all out to make sure that this would be a night that we would both remember.

I spread the red rose petals all over the brand-new comforter set and floor. I had candles surrounding the entire bed, but I wasn't going to light them until right before I left. I had fresh fruit and whipped cream, along with edible oils on the nightstand next to our king-sized bed. I was getting excited just thinking about it. I spent an entire night's pay on everything. I also purchased Troy some new clothes and shoes, as well as underclothes and cologne. I was hoping that, by doing all of this, it would take away the sting of him finding out that his truck had gotten repossessed. He was going to flip out on me whenever I did tell him. I just couldn't afford to keep up with the notes when I was working at the nursing home. Had I been working at the club, it wouldn't have been too much of a strain. If the money kept rolling in on the night shift, I would be able to get him some more transportation in no time.

I took one last look around the room after lighting the candles. I wanted to make sure that everything was perfect, and it was. I grabbed my purse and keys, preparing to go get my man. Even though I'd been with Malik sexually, Troy had been locked up for a few months without any physical contact. Just the thought of what I knew he would do to me had me smiling. Knowing him, he wasn't going to wait until we got home to have sex. That was exactly why I was wearing a short maxi dress, minus the bra and underwear that should have been underneath. If he wanted it right there in front of the prison, it was his for the taking.

I pulled up to the area of the prison where inmates were released and parked across the street from the exit. There were a few other occupied cars waiting for released inmates as well. It was a few minutes after midnight, so I shouldn't have too much longer to wait. Just as soon as the thought left my mind, the steel doors were opened by a correctional officer who was letting the inmates out. A few women hopped out of their cars to greet their men, but I wasn't one of them because I still didn't see Troy.

Most of the people who were waiting were preparing to leave, with the exception of me and one other car. After a few more minutes of waiting, the door opened again and Troy came walking outside, along with another man. They were so deep in conversation that he didn't seem to notice me parked across the street. I honked my horn to alert him of my presence, but he still didn't come over. He raised his finger to let me know that he was coming as he continued with his conversation. He and the other man appeared to be arguing, but I couldn't make out what they were saying from where I was. Maybe I was reading too much into it, but the man he was talking to seemed a bit feminine to me. He kept putting his hands on his hips and rolling his neck like a woman did when she was upset.

Another ten minutes of talking and Troy finally made his way over to the car, followed by the man that he was talking to. I was pissed, but I knew better than to say anything. Troy didn't have a problem putting his hands on me and he didn't care who was around when he did it. He opened the door and slid into the front seat, while his unidentified friend got into the back.

"Hey baby," he said when he sat down.

"Well damn, can I get a hug or a kiss or something?" I asked while looking over at him. He leaned over and gave me a quick peck on the lips like I was his sister instead of his woman. And he never did introduce me to his friend, so I did the honors myself.

"Troy is so rude, but I'm his girlfriend, Keanna," I said smiling at him through my rearview mirror. If looks could kill, I would be the latest victim. He had his arms folded across his chest, looking at me like I said something wrong.

16

"That's my boy, Lee," Troy introduced his rude ass friend. "Baby, look, bring me home to get my truck so I can drop him off home. His girl had to work, so she couldn't come get him."

I was in full panic mode now. I planned to tell Troy about his truck, but I didn't plan on telling him in front of an audience. He was too unpredictable when he got mad. Besides, I didn't mind dropping his friend off wherever he had to go.

"It's cool; I'll drop him off home," I volunteered with a smile. Troy looked at me with a scowl on his face before replying.

"Did I ask you to drop him off? Just bring me to get my truck and I'll bring him home myself."

I didn't get scared easily, but I was terrified right now. I had a feeling that all my hard work was for nothing. This entire night was about to be ruined.

"I just thought that since we were already out here, I could just drop him off. I had some things planned for us tonight. It's been a while since we spent any time together."

"You know what, you're right. You can bring me home because I don't have time for all of this back and forth shit. I live in New Orleans East," Lee snapped at me.

He must not have known that I was not that bitch for him to be talking crazy to. And the fact that he was in my car while he was doing it was just unacceptable. I looked at him through my rearview mirror and saw the attitude all over his face. I couldn't understand why since we'd just met a few minutes ago.

"Where do you live at in the East?" I asked him. Lee was an attractive man, but he had an attitude like a bitch. He kept his arms folded across his chest and his lips were poked out like a little ass girl.

"I live on Bullard in the Wind Run Apartments." Not only did he live all the way out in the East, but he was also in the damn hood. He didn't have to worry about me staying to make sure he got inside. Once I dropped his ass off, he was on his own.

I slowly pulled away from the curb and headed towards the interstate. The sooner I got rid of him, the better. Troy hadn't said much since I started driving and he seemed to be upset for some reason.

"Are you okay?" I asked while looking over at him.

"Man, just drive," he replied angrily.

I wanted to ask him what he was mad about, but I left it alone. The ride to drop Lee off was quiet and full of tension. I couldn't wait until he got out of the car, so Troy and I could have a much-needed talk.

After riding for about twenty minutes, we finally arrived at Lee's apartment. As soon as the car stopped, he jumped out and slammed the door. His ungrateful ass never even bothered to thank me for giving him a ride home.

"What the fuck is his problem?" I asked Troy.

"You better not ever try to talk crazy to me in front of none of my friends again."

"I didn't try to talk crazy to you. I just said that I would bring him home since we were already out here."

"Just do what the fuck I tell you to do next time!" This time, I didn't respond. I knew how far to go with Troy. He had a temper that was like nothing that I'd ever seen before. I pulled off and headed back toward the bridge.

When we pulled up to our house, I wasn't in the mood to do any of the things that I had planned for us. Thanks to Troy's sudden attitude, all of my hard work was for nothing. We walked through the door and the scent of the candles greeted us as soon as we did. The music was on low and the food was staying warm in the oven. Troy looked around, but he didn't acknowledge any of it. He kept going towards the back of the house, crushing all the rose petals with every step he took. When he made it to the bedroom, he flipped on the lights and started blowing out all the candles. I wanted to cry, but I sucked it up, just like every other time.

"Do you want me to fix you something to eat?" I asked. I was trying to get him in a better mood, but that wasn't looking too promising.

"Nope," he replied simply. After taking an outfit out of the closet, he pulled some underwear from his drawer and walked into the bathroom. He never once acknowledged the new clothes and shoes that I bought for him.

"What the fuck is all of this!" he yelled from behind the bathroom door. I went into the bathroom to see what he was referring to.

"Take this shit out of the tub. I can't even take a damn shower in here."

I'd completely forgotten about the rose petals that were floating all over the bathtub. I grabbed the small trashcan from under the sink and started throwing them away. Once I was done, I washed the bathtub and left out.

"I need a cell phone," Troy said as soon as I walked back into the room. He had a phone before he went to jail, but I stopped paying the bill when he left.

"I'll get your old one turned back on tomorrow."

He got up and went back into the bathroom and prepared to take a shower. I went into the kitchen and took the food out of the oven. Then, I turned off the radio and threw away all the candles and rose petals that were strategically placed around the house. If I would have known that it wouldn't have been appreciated, I would have saved my money.

I went back to my bedroom and traded my maxi dress for a pair of pajamas. Going to bed sexually frustrated was nothing new to me. Troy came out of the bathroom wearing only his boxers and that frustrated me even more. He completely ignored me as he got dressed. This nigga hadn't been home for a good hour and he was actually about to leave.

"Where are you going?" I asked.

"I need to make a few moves. Where are my keys?"

At first, I was scared to tell him about his truck but, now, I looked forward to it. With the way he was treating me, nothing would give me greater pleasure. Knowing him, he was probably going to get high on his first day out.

"Keys to what?" I asked nonchalantly.

"What do you mean keys to what? I need the keys to my truck." He looked at me with a frown like I was stupid.

"It ain't here." I looked at the tv screen, refusing to make eye contact with him. He stopped brushing his hair and turned to face me.

"What the fuck you mean it ain't here? Where is it then?"

"The people repossessed it. I couldn't afford to pay the car note anymore. I got a little behind on the payment and they came and got it." That panicked feeling came back to me in no time.

"What! I know you didn't let them people come and take my shit!" he yelled angrily as he ran to the front door.

I got up and ran behind him to see what he was doing. I got to the door just in time to see him looking around the parking lot like a damn fool. He could look all day and night, but it wouldn't bring his truck back. That was a done deal. He rushed back over to me with fire in his eyes and I knew that this night would only get worse.

"I can't believe this shit. You in the club shaking your flat ass all night and you couldn't pay a fucking car note! Where they do that shit at?"

"I was still working at the nursing home when they took it. I just couldn't afford the payments," I cried. He didn't appreciate the little things I did, but his insults hurt more than anything.

"This is some straight bullshit. I don't have a phone or a car. I could've just stayed locked up if I knew I was coming home to this shit!"

Being the damn fool in love that I was, I went into the bedroom and grabbed my phone and car keys. I walked over to where he was sitting and handed them over to him. For the first time since I picked him up from the prison, he smiled.

"Thanks, baby. I need to make some moves to get us some extra money. I promise, we'll spend all day together tomorrow," he said, standing to his feet.

He leaned down and gave me a kiss before he walked out the door. I locked the door behind him and retreated to my bedroom, where I cried myself to sleep yet again.

Chapter 3

I was so sick and tired of crying but that seemed to be all that I did lately. I'd be the first to admit that I made a lot of stupid mistakes and I was paying for them now. Hurting Tyree was the last thing that I wanted to do, but I ended up doing it anyway. I tried calling to apologize, but he would never answer my calls. I couldn't even get mad, especially since I brought all of this on myself.

I was still friends with his sisters, even though they knew what I'd done to their brother. Of course, they didn't agree with it, but they never treated me any different because of it. All my school books and some of my clothes were still at Tyree's house, but he wouldn't let anybody come and get it. He wanted me to be the one to face him and that was no more than right. I had a bad habit of running away from things that I didn't want to face, but he wasn't having it.

Thankfully, I didn't fall behind on my studying, thanks to some of my classmates. Some of them allowed me to use their books to study during their time off from class. Even though I appreciated their kind gestures, it was nothing like having my own.

"How long do you plan on hiding out from the world?" Jada asked as she walked into her living room.

I felt so bad that I got her involved in all of my madness. She kept telling me to leave Dre alone, but my stubborn ass didn't listen. Now, not only did Tyree cut me off, but he was mad with Jada too.

"I'm not hiding out. I leave out of here all the time," I replied.

I'd been at Jada's for the past two weeks. I would have gone home, but I wasn't ready to face my sister just yet. Mainly because I didn't know what I would do to her when I saw her. I expected some low down dirty shit from Keanna, but my own sister was out to get me and I didn't know why. She was the one who supplied the key in order for them to gain entrance into Jada's apartment. Ayanna and I didn't have the best relationship, but I was always there for her and her kids. If she needed money for a bill or anything for her kids, I was always there to lend a helping hand.

"You only leave this house to go to school and you come right back. Don't get me wrong; you're welcomed to stay as long as you want but hiding is not going to make the situation better."

"I keep telling you that I'm not hiding," I lied. I needed to, but I wasn't ready to face anybody right now.

"Well, and this is just my opinion, you need to go get your stuff from Tyree's house. Then, you need to curse Dre's ass out after you whip your sister and Keanna's asses. And you need to do it in that exact order."

She was stuck on the idea of Dre having something to do with all of this, but I didn't know what to believe. He seemed just as surprised as I was when everybody showed up that night. Then, again, I couldn't put anything past Dre. When he wanted something, he had ways of making sure he got it.

"Yeah, you're right. I really do need to go get my books. Sharing books with other people is getting old. And I really need to apologize to Tyree. He might not want to hear it, but I really need to say it. I owe him that much."

"I'm not saying that you're innocent because you played a part in all of this too, but I can't help but feel that Dre is behind all of this. Just think about it, Lex. His car wasn't even parked out front, so how did they know that he was here? The only cars they saw were yours and mine, so he had to tell them where he was."

She was getting hyped up just talking about it. I had to admit that she did have a point. There was no way for anyone to know that Dre was here unless he told them. I knew that asking him was pointless. He would only lie like he always did.

"Well, I guess it's now or never," I said, standing to my feet.

"You want me to come with you?"

"No, I need to handle this on my own. And I want to go talk to my mama about that evil bitch that she gave birth to. She needs to know why I haven't been home for the past two weeks and I'm going to tell her."

"So, are you going by Tyree?"

"Yep, that's going to be my first stop."

I grabbed my keys and purse, preparing to go do one of the hardest things that I'd ever had to do in my life. I was nervous about seeing him again, but I was ready to face my reality.

I got off on the exit that led to Tyree's house with my heart beating twice as fast as it should have been. I didn't know if he was home or not, but I was taking a chance by showing up anyway. It wasn't like I could call to tell him that I was on my way since he wasn't answering the phone for me. When I turned on his street, I saw his car parked in his driveway, but that still didn't mean that he was home. Tyree had two cars and a bike, so he could have been using either one of them.

Still, I parked my car behind his and made my way to the front door. I bowed my head and said a silent prayer right before ringing the doorbell. I prayed that, even if we never got back together, he would at least forgive me. After ringing his doorbell a second time, he finally came to the door. My heart broke into a million pieces when I saw the condition that he was in. Tyree took pride in his appearance, but the man that stood before me had definitely seen better days. His face was unshaven and his hair looked like it hadn't been cut in weeks. His eyes were bloodshot red and I actually saw stains on the front of his t-shirt.

"Hey," I said nervously. "I just came to get my books and stuff if it's okay with you."

He stepped aside and allowed me come in. I looked around the darkened living room and it didn't even look like the same house that I'd spent so much time in before. Clothes were thrown around everywhere and the floor was cluttered with empty liquor bottles. I walked deeper into the house and everything else seemed to be intact.

I guess he spent most of his time in the living room, since that was the only part of the house that looked like a wreck. I walked up the stairs and I felt Tyree walking behind me. I was already nervous, but the feeling was working overtime now. I had a million crazy thoughts running through my head and none of them were good.

As soon as I got to the room, I grabbed my duffel bag out of the closet and started filling it up with all of my clothes and toiletries. Tyree just stood by the door and watched me the entire time I packed. I opened the closet and looked for my back pack, but it wasn't there.

"Um, where is my back pack?" I asked, looking up at him.

"So, that's all that you have to say for yourself?" he asked with a scowl on his face. "I walk in on you in the bed with your ex and you're worried about a fucking back pack!"

I knew that this was coming and this was the reason why I stayed away for so long.

"I asked you if you were happy over and over again, and you sat there and lied to my face," he said while looking at me.

"I didn't lie," I said, lowering my head in guilt. "I was happy; I just made a stupid mistake and I'm sorry."

I wiped the few tears that made their way down my cheeks. Tyree made me very happy so there was no excuse for me messing with Dre.

"You can miss me with all that crying shit. Your tears don't move me at all. If you knew this wasn't what you wanted, you should have said something a long time ago."

"It is what I want. I just made a stupid mistake that I wish I could take back."

"No, what you thought is that you could be a hoe and have both of us, but I guess ole boy wasn't having it. He got a wife, but he doesn't want you to have a boyfriend. Was it that serious for him to be with you that he had to set you up? What kind of nigga does that shit anyway?"

I glared at him with a perplexed look on my face. I know he didn't just say that Dre had set me up. It was one thing to hear it from Jada, but for Tyree to confirm it was another story. I wondered what he knew that I didn't.

"Don't look so surprised. That same nigga that claims to love you so much set your stupid ass up to get busted. As crazy as it sounds, I'm happy that he did or I probably would have never found out that you were a hoe."

I don't think I'd ever felt so low in my life. I knew that Dre was crazy, but this was ridiculous.

"Was it worth it?" Tyree asked out of the blue.

"What?" I countered. He caught me off guard with the question.

"Was being with him worth losing what we had?"

"No and I'm so sorry. I wish I could take it back, but I can't. Even if we never get back together, I just ask for your forgiveness. I never meant to hurt you," I said, reaching out to touch his face.

He backed away from my touch and walked off without replying. I felt so stupid. I couldn't believe that I lost the first man that I was ever really in love with behind Dre's dog ass. Even though he was wrong for setting me up, I couldn't even be mad with him. Saying no to Dre could have easily put a stop to all of this. Tyree walked back into the room carrying my back pack.

"Here," he said, dropping it on the floor in front of me. I picked it up and grabbed my duffle bag from the floor as well. I really wanted to say something else to him, but I didn't really know what to say. I just felt like I didn't have the closure that I needed.

"And just so you know, I'm done with your trifling ass. Don't call or text me for nothing. If you see me, act like you don't even know me. Loyalty is all that I have and you don't seem to know what that is. That's what I get for trying to wife a hoe."

It was as if he was reading my mind. He was giving me the closure that I needed, even though it wasn't what I wanted.

"I am not a hoe," I replied defensively.

"You sure could have fooled me. Honestly, I really don't want to hear nothing else that you have to say. Just get out and stay the fuck away from me."

I knew that he would be upset, but I never thought that I'd hear those words come out of his mouth when it came to me. With teary eyes, I made my way down the stairs and out the front door as quickly as I could. Tyree slammed the door behind me without a second thought. As soon as I got into my car, I broke down into a sea of tears. My life was all fucked up and I wasn't sure how I was going to get it back on track. I pulled my phone from my purse and dialed Jada's number.

"Hey girl," she said after picking up on the first ring. I was crying so hard that I couldn't even talk when she answered.

"Lex!" Jada yelled into the phone. "What's wrong? Did something happen?"

"No," I cried. "Well, Tyree broke up with me, but I expected that. It's just the way he said it that hurt the most. But, you were right; Dre was in on it the whole time."

"I knew it! I told you that I didn't trust his stalking ass. He was that pressed that he had to do some shit like that?"

"I don't know, but I swear on my life that I'm done with his ass. I can't believe he did me like that."

"Well, he damn sure didn't act alone. Keanna and your sister are just as guilty as he is. I can't believe I forgot to get my key back from that bitch, Ayanna."

"It's all good though. I got something for both of them bitches whenever I see them. I'm down, but I'm not out."

"I know that's right friend. And you already know that I got your back."

"I know. It'll be funny to see you fighting your two ex-girlfriends," I said laughing.

"Very funny heifer. I'm happy to hear you laughing, even if the joke is on me," Jada said, laughing with me.

"Well, I'll see you later. I'm about to go talk to my mama," I told Jada before disconnecting our call.

Things were bad, but I knew that they could be worse. I backed out of Tyree's driveway and made my way over to my mother's house.

As soon as I turned on my mama's street and looked towards her house, my blood started to boil. It took everything in me not to turn around when I saw Ayanna's car parked out front. Running away from my problems was one thing but running away from a fight was not happening. No doubt about it, I planned to whip her ass and I wasn't changing my mind on that. I just didn't want to do her dirty in my mama's house and especially not in front of her kids.

"Mama!" I yelled when I walked through the front door. I heard the tv, so I figured they were sitting in the dining room. I started walking that way when my mama appeared in the doorway.

"Hey stranger, I haven't seen you in forever," my mama said, pulling me in for a hug. She knew that I was at Jada's house because I called her every day to let her know that I was alright. I was the youngest of six and she still referred to me as her baby.

"It smells good in here. What are you cooking?"

"I made some shrimp pasta for the kids, but there's more than enough if you want some."

"Let me put all of this stuff up first and I'll be back down. I want to talk to you about something."

I headed up the stairs to unpack my belongings. I unlocked my bedroom door and looked around my spacious room. Since Ayanna and her kids moved in, my mama got locks put on both of our bedroom doors to keep my nieces and nephews out of our rooms. I unpacked all of my things that I took from Tyree's house and put everything away. After I ate and talked to my mama, I wanted to take a shower and get in my books for the rest of the night. I loved chilling at Jada's house, but I missed being in my own space.

When I was done in my room, I went back downstairs to the kitchen. I was so depressed lately and I hadn't eaten a real meal in a few days. I would eat some fruit or yogurt throughout the day, but that was about it.

"Hey Lex," my nieces said when I walked into the kitchen. They were seated at the kitchen table, eating the food that their grandmother fixed for them.

"Hey, my babies," I replied, speaking back to them. I walked to the cabinet and pulled out a plate, preparing to fix myself something to eat.

"So, what did you want to talk to me about?" my mama asked me.

Before I could reply, Ayanna walked her retarded looking ass into the kitchen. She looked at me with that stupid ass smirk on her face and it took everything in me not to lay her ass out right there in the kitchen. She fixed herself a plate and sat down in one of the kitchen chairs and started eating.

"Talk to me, Lex; what's up?" My mama looked at me like she was waiting for me to say what was on my mind.

"I'll talk to you later; I'm going to my room."

Just that fast, my appetite was gone. Just the sight of my sister had me feeling some kind of way. I sat my plate down and started walking out of the kitchen.

"What's up play girl, you not speaking?" Ayanna asked sarcastically, with that smirk that I hated so much. That was all that I needed to hear. I was already on fire and she just added fuel to the already burning inferno. I turned around just as quickly as I left and delivered a blow to her face that made her fall backwards in her chair.

"Oh, my God! Alexus! Stop!" my mother screamed. My nieces started screaming too, but that didn't stop me from beating the brakes off of their mama.

"Y'all go upstairs!" my mama yelled to the kids. They jumped up and did as they were told. When Ayanna fell back in her chair, I pounced on her like a wounded animal. Every lick that I threw met with a different part of her body and I didn't care about which part it hit.

"Alexus, stop this. What is wrong with you?" My mama was crying and that was something that I hated to see. I felt bad for doing this in front of her, but some things just couldn't be helped. I kept throwing blow after blow, while Ayanna tried to cover her already blood-stained face. After what seemed like forever, my mama was finally able to pull me off of her. And just like always, Ayanna jumped up and was still talking shit, bloody mouth, and all.

"Fuck you, Alexus. Dre don't love your stupid ass. Who do you think set everything up?" she cried.

"Set what up? What are you talking about?" my mama asked.

"Yeah, tell her what your hating ass did. Tell her how you helped a nigga set your own sister up to get busted. Ole jealous hearted bitch!" I was out of breath as I yelled at her.

She ignored me and walked over to the counter to get some paper towels for her face.

"Somebody better tell me something," my mama said, looking back and forth between us.

Since I knew that Ayanna wasn't going to talk, I started telling my mama everything that happened, not holding out on one detail. I even told her about Ayanna messing with Jada and working in a strip club. I told her about me cheating on Tyree with Dre and everything else that took place over the past few months. When I was done talking, my poor mama had to take a seat.

"What is wrong with you?" my mama asked while looking up at Ayanna.

"Why are you always taking her side? No matter what happens, Alexus is always right and everybody else is wrong!" Ayanna yelled.

"Well, in this case, you are wrong. You don't go against your family for nobody. We're supposed to help and not hurt each another, Ayanna. I thought I taught you better than that." My mama sounded so hurt and I knew exactly how she felt.

"Fuck her!" Ayanna spat angrily.

"Get out!" my mama yelled at my sister.

"What?" Ayanna replied.

"You heard me. Get your shit and get the fuck out of my house. I didn't think that I would ever see the day where something I brought into this world could be so damned evil. You are jealous and hateful, and you will not tear this family apart with your evil ways."

"Fuck you! Me and my kids will live under the bridge before we stay here another day."

My mama jumped up and grabbed me when she saw that I was going after Ayanna again. It was one thing for her to curse me out, but to do it to my mama was unacceptable.

"No Alexus, let it go," my mama begged.

My mama had her faults, but she didn't deserve to be talked to like that. I took a step back and stood against the kitchen door so that I could see Ayanna's every move.

"You can go be homeless by yourself, but you are not taking those kids out of this house with nowhere to go." My mama loved her grandkids so I wasn't surprised by what she said.

She never wanted to be bothered with her kids anyway, so I was sure that she wasn't going to put up too much of a fight. I still couldn't believe that she cursed my mama out, after all that she tried to do to help her. My mama made sure that her kids went to bed clean and full every night. She made sure that they got to and from school on time. They always had food in the house, even if she didn't cook every day, and this was the thanks she got. With a wad of wet paper towels covering her face, Ayanna stormed out of the kitchen and ran up the stairs.

"I'm sorry for fighting in your house," I said, walking over to my mama.

She looked up at me with tears in her eyes and I really felt bad about everything that happened.

"I know that I'm not the best mother in the world. I've had my share of men too, but you're better than that Alexus. Don't make the same mistakes that I made. You can't think that what you did is okay because it's not. Dre is poison and he poisons everything that he touches. I'm just sorry that you had to find out the hard way."

Just as she finished talking, Ayanna came walking down the steps with a duffel bag full of clothes. She walked into the kitchen and threw the house key on the table before turning around and walking out of the front door.

"The streets are going to kill her," my mama said while getting up to lock the door behind her.

As mad as I was at my sister, I prayed that my mother's prediction was wrong. I would be devastated if something were to happen to her.

After cleaning the mess that was made in my mama's kitchen, I retreated to my room and prepared to study. My grades were almost perfect, since studying was the most fun that I'd had in the past few weeks.

Chapter 4

I had to be about the dumbest nigga in the world to let Keanna play me the way she did. Crazy thing was, I knew how Keanna thought. She would use who or whatever she could use to make something happen. It just so happened that she used me this time. I'd be the first to admit that I wasn't thinking clearly. I loved Alexus so much that I was willing to do anything to be with her. The problem was, I made things even worse. I assumed that, when things went left with her and her new man, she would come running back to me, but she did the exact opposite of what I wanted her to do. I called her all day, every day, but she never answered. After a few days of calling, she ended up blocking me altogether.

To say that I was sick was an understatement. I was so desperate that I even tried calling Jada's ole hating ass. She made sure that she answered each time I called, just to tell me off. I knew Alexus better than anyone else and I saw that she really did love this Tyree dude. Knowing that was just too much for me to handle. I wasn't trying to let her be happy with nobody else if it wasn't me.

I saw her car parked by her mama a few times, but I never went over there. Alexus' mama was crazy and I was her least favorite person in the world. She wouldn't hesitate to call the police on me. I even went as far as following her one day, but I lost sight of her when she pulled up at school and got out of the car. I knew that, if I just talked to her, I could make everything alright with us. She could resist me over the phone, but she couldn't resist me in person, no matter how hard she tried.

I pulled myself away from my troubled thoughts when I pulled up to Cherika's house. I'd been so busy stalking Lex that I hadn't spent any time with my kids for over a week. I didn't even call to check on them, so hearing Cherika's mouth was unavoidable. I rang the doorbell and waited for somebody to let me in. I used to have a key to the house that I once shared with my wife but, when Alexus found out, she had a fit, prompting me to give it back.

"Hey daddy," Denim said, jumping into my arms.

"Daddy!" Dream yelled excitedly as she ran over to me, almost knocking me down.

"Hey, my baby girls." I picked them up and made my way over to the sofa. I felt bad for staying away from them that long. I hadn't been in the best mood, but that was not an excuse. Whatever I was going through was not their fault.

"Hey Dre," Cherika said when she walked into the living room with Lil Dre and Drew.

I had to do a double take when I saw her. She had on a long black dress with red strips. The red heels and jewelry that she wore complemented her outfit very well. Cherika had perfect dark chocolate skin so, besides lip gloss, she didn't wear much make-up. Her hair was braided, but it was pulled up into a bun and she wore it very well.

36

"Hey Cherika. How you been?" I asked her.

"I've been fine and yourself?" I was almost at a loss for words. I was so use to her biting my head off whenever I was here. I was shocked to actually be holding a normal conversation with her.

"I can't complain."

"That's good. But, you never told me how long they were staying with you, so they have 2 days' worth of clothes. If they need more, just let me know and I'll pack them some. I have class the day after tomorrow, so I'd appreciate if you could keep them until then."

I was just sitting there staring at the stranger that was standing in front of me. It was only about two months ago that she was threatening to kill me and Alexus because I didn't come get the kids like I promised. Now, she was standing here acting like she was my best friend.

"That's not a problem; I'll keep them for a few days and give you a break."

"Thanks," she said with a smile on her face.

I didn't know where this new Cherika came from, but I didn't mind being around her, as long as she was calm like this. She hadn't been on my back about going back to counseling or about us getting back together. I was starting to wonder if there was another man in the picture. Even though Cherika and I were separated, I didn't know how I felt about her being with somebody else.

"You look nice. Are you going on a date or something?" I asked, trying to feel her out. I laughed a little, but I was serious.

"No. I'm going somewhere with my mama. Besides, I'm still married, so I can't go on a date, even if I wanted to." I guess she was throwing that cheap shot at me, but I didn't respond to it.

"Well, we're about to go. I'll let them call you tomorrow," I said right before walking out the front door.

After securing all four of my kids in the car, we made our way over to my mama's house. I was on my way to pick up my brother, Eric, since he was staying the night at my house as well. We hadn't hung out in a while and it was long overdue. My mama and sisters weren't home, so I didn't bother getting out of the car. When I blew my horn, Eric came out, locked the door, and jogged over to my truck.

"What's up Little Rascals?" he said to my kids when he slid into the passenger's seat.

"Nigga, stop playing with my kids before I make them jump your ass." Eric didn't have any kids, but he was always good with his nieces and nephews.

"What are we drinking tonight man? Let's stop and load up before we go in," Eric said, reading my mind.

"Yeah, I promised to get them some snacks, so I need to stop somewhere."

After spending over an hour in Wal-Mart, we were on our way back to my condo. Between my kids grabbing toys and snacks and me and Eric grabbing liquor, I spent over two hundred dollars, but I wasn't complaining.

"Aye, stop me at the gas station up here so I can get me some cigars," Eric requested as we approached a Shell station. I pulled up to a pump, deciding to fill my tank up since we were here. Once Eric got what he needed, he came walking back to the car with a smirk on his face.

"Man, you not gon' believe who I just ran into in there."

"Who?" I asked curiously.

"That nigga Troy is in there begging me for something to drink and shit."

When he said that, I began to look around the parking lot for his truck, but I didn't see it. When I looked on the other side of the pumps, I saw Keanna's car backed into a spot near the exit, so she must have been in the store with him. I didn't even know that he was home, but I was happy that I found out.

"Is Keanna in there with him?"

"No. He was in there with some other dude."

"Damn man, I'm sorry that I got my kids with me. I want to put my foot up his ass so bad."

"Nah, you can't do that with your babies around. You gon' get your chance to get at him."

We both hopped in the truck and was about to pull off when Troy came strolling out of the store, followed by another man who looked familiar. I looked long and hard at the man that he was walking with until I figured out who he was.

"Get the fuck out of here!" I yelled as he walked away with Lee walking right behind him.

Lee was known as the diva of Orleans Parish Prison. He dressed like a man but did everything else like a female. According to Quan, Troy had been moved off of several dorms because he always got into fights with somebody over Lee.

"What?" Eric asked, looking over at me.

"That's the dude that he was fucking with when we were locked up."

"That nigga gay?" Eric asked, shocked by the information that he'd just received.

"What does it look like to you?" I gestured at the two men with my hand.

"Man, I can't believe this shit. Keanna likes girls and her man is into boys. They really are made for each other."

Troy and Lee hopped in Keanna's car and sped out of the gas station's parking lot. He had Lee riding in the front seat of his girl's car like it was no big deal. It was sad to say, but I didn't feel sorry for Keanna at all. It was crazy how she stayed up in other people's business but couldn't see what was going on right before her eyes.

Chapter 5

After months and months of begging, my mama was finally able to convince me to go to church with her and I've been nothing but grateful ever since. I was far from being whole again, but I felt so much better when I was there. I could tell that everybody in the congregation already knew all my business, thanks to my nosey ass mama. As soon as I walked through the doors for the first time, all eyes were on me. I could tell that they felt sorry for me, but I didn't need to be a guest at nobody's pity party, including my own. The First Lady pulled me to the side and prayed for me with the help of my mother and the ushers. When I left that night, I was soaking wet with holy oil, holy water and my own tears.

For the past few weeks, I'd been going to their weekly women's meetings and I looked forward to them now. They helped me to understand why Dre did the things that he did to me. It was because I allowed him to do it.

They helped me to know that a man who truly loved his wife would never do the things that he did to me. I was so busy placing all the blame on Alexus; I never gave Dre's actions a second thought. Truth was, he was just as guilty. He was the one who took vows with me, so he was even guiltier than Alexus.

I still loved my husband to death but going to the meetings at church taught me that I should love myself just as much or even more. I would have my GED in three months and I still refrained from drinking any alcohol.

At first, I was changing my ways to win Dre back, but now everything that I was doing was for my children and me. I wanted more and they deserved more from me. I could tell that my change in attitude shocked Dre. He was so used to me calling him all day and arguing with him whenever he came over, but I was getting tired of doing that. Dre was always going to do whatever he wanted to do, no matter who got hurt in the process. It was just unfortunate that I was the only one who was always getting hurt. Even though I knew what my husband was capable of, I still didn't know how I felt about us getting divorced. Dre still had a hold on my heart but, with each passing day, the grip wasn't as tight as it was the day before.

"I know I don't tell you this that often, but I'm so proud of you," my mama said, smiling at me.

We had just come back from one of the meetings at the church and was now sitting in her dining room, eating the food that she prepared. She was so happy to see the changes in me, especially since she was the one who always encouraged me to change.

"Thanks Ma, I'm trying," I replied proudly. It'd been a while since I had my head on straight, but it felt good. I was actually seeing how it felt to put me and my kids first and not Dre.

"So, are you going to file for a divorce now?"

"Don't start Ma. I haven't even thought that far ahead yet. I still love my husband; I'm just learning how to love me as well."

I could tell that she didn't like my answer, but it was the only one that I could give her. I was being as honest as I could be. I spent most of my adult life being in love with Dre, so it was impossible to turn it off in a matter of days. I wasn't sure if my love for him would ever go away.

"Well, I think you should give it some more thought. You said yourself that nothing with him has changed. He's still chasing behind that same little girl, instead of trying to make things right with his wife."

It never failed. No matter what I did or tried to do, it was never good enough for my mother. Her hate for Dre almost outweighed her love for me.

"I don't understand how you call yourself a woman of God and walk around with hate in your heart."

She stopped eating and looked at me with a surprised looked covering her face. Maybe I'd gone too far with what I said, but she needed to hear it. For years, I'd watched my mother walk around with a smile plastered on her face for the world to see, but she was a different person behind closed doors. She hated my husband and it affected our relationship as mother and daughter because of that.

"I don't have hate in my heart for anybody, Cherika. As a mother, you don't know what it does to me to see you unhappy and crying all the time. For years, I've sat back and watched while you turned into somebody that I no longer knew. The life was sucked out of you right before my very eyes, and you want to me to embrace the man that's responsible for doing it to you. I'm sorry, but I just can't do that."

"I'm not asking you to embrace him. I'm just asking you to respect whatever decision I make, rather I stay with him or not. It's hard enough being judged by everyone else in the world. I can't take being judged by you too."

"Exactly how am I judging you? The problem is you get mad when I point out the facts. Dre is and always has been selfish, and I told you that before you even married him. It's always about what he wants and nobody else. He doesn't think like a married man because he doesn't want to be married."

"You might be right but, at the end of the day, the decision is not yours to make. I just need you to be here for me in whatever I decide to do."

"I'm always here for you and I always will been. I just hope you make the right decision this time. Don't let him sweet talk his way back into your life, only for him to hurt you again. You might think that you can handle it, but everybody gets tired. You're human and you can only take so much," my mama said in her usual concerned voice.

I lowered my head and continued to eat my food without responding. I knew without a doubt that my mama loved me and wanted what was best for me and my kids. There were times when I was at my lowest point and she was the only one who was there for me. When my sisters and I stopped speaking because of Dre, she never turned her back on me, and I loved her for that and so much more. For the next hour, we made small talk while we ate. When we were done, I helped my mother clean up her kitchen before I left to go home. The kids had been with Dre for the past three days and they were finally coming home tonight.

It was a little after ten when I made it to my house. I called Dre when I was on my way and told him that he could be on his way with the children. I knew they would be tired, so I was happy when he told me that he'd already given them a bath. Dre might have been a terrible husband, but he was a dream come true when it came down to our kids.

That wasn't really a shock to me though because kids were his weakness. Actually, kids and women were his weaknesses. I was both surprised and pleased to know that my kids were the only ones that he'd fathered. With as many women that he'd been with, he never had any outside kids. That was something that I didn't think I could've handled. I

44

knew I was wrong for feeling that way, especially since Drew wasn't his, but I couldn't help it.

I was cleaning my kitchen when the ringing of my doorbell got my attention. I opened the door to find Dre carrying a sleeping Drew in his arms.

"What's up?" Dre asked, walking into the house followed by the kids. They looked like they were worn out and ready for bed.

"Hey," I replied while looking him up and down. I had to keep reminding myself not to go there with him again. I was like a recovering addict who was trying hard not to relapse. It was getting harder and harder for me to be around him, but I couldn't avoid it. He walked up the steps, carrying Drew to his bedroom.

"Y'all come on and get in the bed!" he called out to the other kids. They must have really been tired because they followed behind him without putting up a fight. I went back into the kitchen and continued to clean, while Dre tended to them. He was upstairs for about ten minutes and I never heard him come down but, when I turned around, he was in the doorway staring at me.

"You scared me," I said as I jumped and held my chest. He didn't respond; he just stood there looking at me. "What? Why are you looking at me like that?"

He still didn't say anything, but he walked up and stood directly in front of me. I tried to hold my breath, so I wouldn't smell the Ralph Lauren cologne that he always wore. My heart started beating out of my chest when he leaned down close to me. I closed my eyes as tight as I could as his soft lips connected with the side of my neck. It felt so good; I wanted to melt right there on my kitchen floor. I couldn't believe it. After months and months of begging, my husband was finally ready to give me the attention that I had been craving from him. The only problem was that I was scared to accept it. I couldn't take having him on a temporary basis. Dre knew that I loved hard. If I couldn't have all of him, I wasn't settling for pieces anymore.

"Dre, stop," I protested weakly.

Completely ignoring me, he pinned me against the sink and continued planting soft kisses all over my face and neck.

"Dre, stop. You know that this is not what you want, so stop trying to lead me on. I can't go through any more drama with you. My heart can't take it." I tried my best to push him away from me.

"Why do you have to overthink everything? Just go with the flow sometimes."

I knew right then and there that sex was all that he wanted from me at the moment. I wasn't surprised by that, but I was curious as to why he wanted it from me all of a sudden. I knew for a fact that he was still dealing with Alexus and God knows who else he had on the side. Yet, he was here trying to find his way back into my bed.

"So, it's all about sex with you? You don't have any interest in trying to fix our marriage, do you?"

"Yes, I do, but it's not gon' happen overnight," he replied while sliding his hand up my dress.

"So, what about Alexus?"

"What about her?" He sounded aggravated but I needed some answers. I could tell that this was a conversation that he'd rather not have right now, but I needed to know before we went any further.

Before I had a chance to reply, I felt Dre slip his middle finger into my warm hole. I bit my bottom lip to suppress the moan that was threating to escape. For the past two years, intimacy with Dre mostly consisted of me giving him oral sex. To have him actually take his time and include some type of foreplay was a welcomed and pleasant surprise. I lifted my leg and moved myself up and down, enjoying the sensation that my husband was giving, even if it was temporary. When he saw that I was really into it, he slipped another finger inside of me and I almost lost my mind.

"Mommy, I'm scared," a small voice said from behind us. Dre and I jumped and tried to regain our composure when Drew walked into the kitchen. I pulled my dress down and rushed over to see about my baby. I picked him up and carried him to the living room. Drew was afraid of the dark, so it was no surprise that he came to look for me when he woke up alone in his semi-darkened bedroom.

After a few minutes, Dre came out of the kitchen and headed for the front door.

"I'll talk to you later," he said as he opened the front door.

"You don't have to leave if you don't want to," I replied, sounding more desperate than I wanted to.

"Nah, I got some things to handle, Come lock your door." He left without so much as a backwards glance.

I got up with Drew still in my arms and locked the door behind him. I was so disappointed in myself for even wanting him to stay in the first place. If I wasn't careful, I knew that I would slip right back into the same dark place that I was in before. Why did he have to want me when I was trying so hard to get over him? I really wanted to talk to somebody about how I was feeling, but I didn't know who to call. Dre was trying to get into my head again and I didn't know how to stop it. My mama always told me to talk to God whenever I felt like there was no one else to lean on, so that's exactly what I did. I closed my eyes and prayed that God would lead me in the right direction. Right now, I didn't know if that direction was going back to Dre or away from him, but only time would tell.

Chapter 6

It took me a minute, but I was finally able to bounce back. I couldn't lie; I missed Alexus like crazy, but I couldn't be with somebody that I didn't trust. Even though I told her not to call or text me, she still did it anyway. I never answered any of her calls or replied to any of her text messages. I almost answered for her one time but, when the image of her having sex with her ex came to me, she went unanswered once again. I decided to throw myself into my work to keep my mind off of my troubles.

We had a lot of new clients and I was taking on as many of them as possible. Two clients in particular that I wanted to be done with were Kayla and her mother. Over the past few months, I'd shown them a total of eight buildings and they still hadn't decided on one yet. They claimed that they were interested in building number three, but they wanted to see it again before making a final decision. This time, I told my pops to meet us over here. If anybody could sell them on buying a building, he was just the man to do it. I knew when he got here, I was going to hear his mouth.

The unfortunate part about me and Alexus' breakup was the close relationship that she had with my family. They all felt that we should sit down and talk some more, but that wasn't happening. It was over and I was done talking. I wasn't the one who did anything wrong.

I pulled up to the building that we were showing to Kayla's mama and Kayla was already parked out front. My pops was coming from another appointment, so I knew it would be a minute before he got there. I didn't know where Kayla's mother was because she was in the car by herself. After a few minutes, Kayla got out of her car and walked over to the driver's side of mine. She smiled while motioning for me to roll down my window.

"Hey," she said once the glass was no longer separating us.

"Hey. I thought your mama was supposed to be coming with you."

"She's coming. She had a doctor's appointment, so she'll be in her own car."

I really took a good look at Kayla. She was kind of on the heavy side, but she had a nice shape. She wasn't what I called pretty, but she had some very attractive features. If she wasn't on some crazy stalker shit, we probably could have gone further than we did when we messed around a while ago.

"It's too damn hot out here," Kayla said, fanning her face with her hand. I had my air conditioner on, so I knew that was my cue to invite her into my car. I was about to ask her why the hell did she get out of her car in the first place, but I decided against it.

"You can come and sit in here if you want to."

I didn't have to offer twice. She damn near broke her neck running to the passenger's side of my car to get in.

"Thanks for the invite."

I nodded my head as my response. For about ten minutes, we sat side by side in silence until Kayla decided to strike up a conversation.

"Can I ask you a question?"

"You just did," I replied nonchalantly. I wasn't in the mood for all that talking.

"No, that's not what I wanted to ask you. What happened to us?" she asked, looking over at me. I had a million answers to that question, but all of them would have hurt her feelings. Instead of doing that, I took the easy way out.

"I just wasn't ready to settle down at that time. You didn't seem to understand that." That was partially true. That and the fact that her ass was a nut job was what kept me from being with her.

"I understood; I just really liked you. Well, I guess settling down is not an issue anymore since you have a girlfriend."

"I had a girlfriend. I'm solo and I'm not looking to get into nothing anytime soon." I threw that out there, so she didn't get any ideas in her crazy little head.

"I'm sorry to hear that," she said without an ounce of sincerity.

"Nah, you not sorry to hear it, but thanks anyway."

"I see you're still as outspoken as you were before." I ignored her and started playing with my phone.

"So, since you're single, that means that we can hang out sometimes, right?" Kayla started moving her hand up and down the crotch of my jeans. Any other time I would have stopped her, but I wanted to see just how far this was going to go.

"Hang out and do what?"

I looked down at her hand, not bothering to move it. She was now fumbling with the buckle on my belt, trying to take it loose. Once that was done, she unbuttoned my pants and reached down into my underwear. She licked her full lips seductively when she pulled my semi-hard erection out and looked at it.

After a few slow hand strokes, she had me standing at full attention. In a split second, she leaned over and took as much of me in her mouth as she could. I put my hand on the back of her head and helped to guide it up and down, as her warm mouth took me to another world. I almost forgot how good Mikayla's head game was, but she was giving me a damn good reminder right now. As much as I'd been stressing over the past few weeks, this stress reliever was just what I needed.

"Damn," I moaned in pleasure as she sucked faster. I felt my release coming as I pulled and grabbed a handful of her hair.

"What the fuck!" I heard, followed by tapping on my window.

Kayla and I both jumped at the loud noise. When I opened my eyes, I was met by my father's disapproving glare. He shook his head and kept walking towards the building. I rushed and tried to get myself together as best as I could, while Kayla fixed her hair and applied some gloss to her lips. She had a look of pure embarrassment covering her face.

"Sorry, I didn't see your dad coming," she said shyly.

"It's cool. Let me go talk to him. Just come on in when your mama gets here," I told her right before I exited the car. As soon as I walked into the building, my pops started going off on me.

"What the fuck is wrong with you, boy? You're barely out of one relationship and you're trying to jump into something else." He had an incredulous look on his face but he had it all wrong.

"I'm not trying to start nothing with her. She knows that I'm not looking for anything serious."

"I can't tell with the way she had her whole face buried in your crotch! And then you know that her ass is crazy as shit. I don't understand why you're even going there with her again."

"I'm not dealing with her like that anymore. She started with me and I damn sure wasn't about to stop her," I replied defensively.

I was a single man, so he was crazy if he thought that I was turning down some free head.

"Alright dumb ass, don't say that I didn't warn you. Don't call me when you wake up and find a rabbit boiling on your stove."

My pops had a way with words, but he was right. I had to make sure that Kayla knew where we stood. Lex and I weren't together anymore, but I would be lying if I said that I didn't still love her. I wasn't trying to rush into anything else, especially with Kayla. Right now, I couldn't offer her anything more than sex. If she wanted anything else, I was the wrong man for the job.

Chapter 7

After a few weeks of begging and pleading, I finally convinced Troy to come and watch me dance. When he was in jail, he promised that he would, but he must have had a change of heart when he got out. I was pissed when I found out that he invited two of his cousins to come with him. I wanted him to come alone so that Ayanna and I could give him a private show. As of a few weeks ago, she'd been staying with us since her mother put her out. Troy didn't seem to mind and they got along fine. She stayed out of our way most of the time, so she wasn't a problem.

However, Troy's friend, Lee, was. They were always together. If Troy wasn't at his house, he was at ours. Just about everywhere that Troy went, he had to be following behind him. I didn't know who his girl was, but I knew for a fact that they weren't spending any time together. Troy would get pissed whenever I said something about it, so I just left it alone. We were in a decent place as far as our relationship and I wanted to keep it that way.

"Are you sure that you want your man to come see you dance?" Ayanna asked me as we picked out our outfits for the night.

"I don't care if he sees me dance on the main stage. I really want him to see our private show," I responded with a smirk.

"You don't think he's going to get mad?"

"Hell no. You don't know Troy like I do. If anything, he'll want to join in," I replied, laughing. Although Ayanna and I were attracted to each other, we never did anything outside of our private shows. It's not that I didn't want to; I just wanted her to make the first move. She seemed to be into me just as much as I was into her.

"I'm not trying to cross the line with your man like that. I appreciate him letting me crash with y'all, but I don't want to ruin our friendship and make anybody feel uncomfortable."

"Girl, Troy and I have been together since forever and we've done a little bit of everything over the years. He's not going anywhere and neither am I. We just like to have fun, whether it's just us two or if we invite some company."

Ayanna looked at me sideways, but I was being honest with her. I didn't have anything to hide as far as my sexuality. Troy knew about my attraction to women and he was perfectly fine with it. He had no problem with me bringing other women home, as long as he got to join in on the action.

Once we decided on what we were wearing for the night, we got dressed and applied some light make-up to our faces.

"So, what room did you book for our private show?"

"The usual one." I smiled making her smile in return.

56

The strip club that we worked in had three private rooms, but only one came equipped with a wall mirror and pole.

"Cool, well, I'm going to the main stage. Just let me know whenever you're ready," she said. I nodded my head in response. I really didn't want to go out on the main stage, but I needed the money. After taking a few sips from my bottle of Hennessy, I applied another coat of lip gloss and made my way out to the front of the club.

Two hours and one hundred twenty dollars later, I was running off the main stage. There was a large crowd of people there, but the money wasn't coming in like it usually did. I was ready to call it a night once Ayanna and I did a few private shows. I knew that Troy didn't have any money to pay us, but I was hoping that the other patrons did. I saw him and his cousins in the crowd, and they appeared to be having a good time. Of course, I had to use some of my tip money to make sure he had something to drink since his ass was always broke.

"Girl, the tips are really flowing out there tonight," Ayanna exclaimed excitedly as she came to the back room to count her money.

"Hurry up and do that. We only have about ten minutes before we have to go," I replied anxiously. I sat and watched as Ayanna counted over three hundred dollars in tips, much more than what I made. To say that I was pissed was an understatement. She had been out there the same amount of time as me, but she had cleaned up.

"Ok, I'm done, let's go," she said after she locked her money in her locker. We made our way through the crowd to the private rooms at the back of the club.

"I'm so nervous." Ayanna grabbed my hand, trying her best to relax.

"Why? We do this all the time. It's just Troy. You don't have any reason to be scared."

When I opened the door to the private room, I wanted to turn around and forget the whole thing. Troy wasn't in the room alone, like I instructed him to be. He had both of his cousins in there waiting to see the free show as well. I looked at him and he stared right back at me like he didn't care if I was mad or not.

"I'm not doing this with all of them watching. I thought you said that Troy was going to be by himself," Ayanna whispered nervously.

"He was supposed to be."

"What are y'all waiting for?" Troy asked nonchalantly.

"She doesn't want to dance since you didn't come by yourself like you were supposed to," I said with an attitude.

"You scared of me, baby girl? Come here, I don't bite unless you're into that kind of thing," Troy said while motioning towards the empty space next to him for Ayanna to sit down.

I didn't wait for her to move before I rushed over and took the seat that she was being offered. Ayanna was uncomfortable and it showed all over her face. Even though she was staying with us for a little while, she never really had any interactions with Troy. Either he wasn't home or we would be at the club. But, it was something about the way he looked at her that didn't sit too well with me.

"Man, we're going back out front. You had us thinking that we were about to see some action," Troy's cousin said as they got up and headed out of the room. Ayanna was still standing there looking like a scared child.

"Come sit down baby girl, or are you leaving too?" Troy asked her.

"Um, I'm about to go. I have to drop some money off to my mama for my kids. I'll see you later Keanna," she said right before she rushed out of the room. I didn't blame her for running away since Troy was damn near undressing her with his eyes.

"What was up with all that baby girl shit?" I snapped as soon as we were left alone.

58

"As long as you live, you better not ever question me again. You need to be happy that I'm even letting you breathe after your trifling ass had the nerve to have another nigga in my house," he spat angrily.

My palms started sweating as nervous energy took over my entire body. I thought my fling with Malik would be a secret that I took to my grave, but Troy had somehow found out and I didn't know how.

"What are you talking about? I never had anybody in your house." I stammered as I tried to lie my way out of it. He grabbed my arm and twisted it behind my back until I cried out in pain.

"Well, then, tell me how the fuck I found this wedged in between the sofa!" he yelled as he threw something at me.

I picked up what he had thrown and my eyes widened in surprise. It was Malik's debit card. I remembered the day he lost it. We searched the entire house and still came up empty, so it baffled me that Troy was the one who found it. The card had been cancelled months ago, but it was still proof of Malik's presence in the home.

"Speechless, huh?" Troy asked with sarcasm dripping from his voice. And I was. There was no reason that I could give that was good enough as to why another man's debit card was found in our home.

"Baby, it wasn't even like that," I said, attempting to explain myself. He raised his hand to stop me from talking.

"It's all good. No need to explain," he said, standing to his feet. I knew better than to think that everything was alright. Troy was not the forgiving type. He was going to hold this over my head as an excuse for whenever he did something wrong. I jumped in front of the door before he had a change to leave.

"Please, just sit down so we can talk about it."

"Nah, we're good," he said as he pushed me out of the way and walked out.

I wanted to cry, but I'd brought all of this on myself. When I started messing with Malik, it was only to piss Alexus off. I never thought that I'd develop feelings for him, but I did. Even though I cared for him a lot, it wasn't enough to lose Troy over him. And to make matters worse, I didn't have a clue as to how he felt about me. Even now, when we hooked up, I had to meet him around the corner from his sister's house like I wasn't good enough to come to the front door. He always gave me some lame ass excuse about not wanting her in his business, but I didn't buy that at all.

I pulled myself away from my troubles and prepared to call it a night. I walked into the almost empty locker room and took off my costume. After getting dressed, I grabbed all my belongings and headed for the back door. I didn't know what kind of mood Troy was going to be in when I got home. He was back to his old drug habit, so his mood swings were always so unpredictable. It was a little after two in the morning, so the parking lot was fairly empty with the exception of a few cars. Mine was parked all the way to the end of the lot, so I made my way to it as quickly as I could. Right before I got to the spot where I was parked, I felt someone walking closely behind me. My first instinct was to grab the can of mace or the Taser from my purse, but it was already too late. My hair was pulled from behind and a series of punches soon followed. I dropped everything that I was holding as I tried desperately to protect myself.

"You know what bitch; I don't want to attack you from behind. Turn around, so you can see who's beating that ass!" my attacker yelled.

It didn't surprise me at all when I turned around and came face to face with Alexus. After what I had done to her, I was surprised that she didn't come for me sooner.

She was dressed in leggings and tennis shoes, so I knew that she came prepared to fight. I'd seen Alexus in action enough times to know that this was one fight that I had no chance of winning. Even still, I was prepared to defend myself as she charged me once again with blows hard enough to weaken the strongest man.

Each time she threw a lick, it met with some part of my body, but she concentrated mostly on my face. I tasted the blood inside my mouth and the ringing in my ears was sure to last for days to come. Even though I was swinging like my life depended on it, I had yet to hit anything. After a devastating blow to my stomach, I went down to the ground since all the wind was knocked right out of me. The face numbing kicks came soon after and I prayed that it would end soon. I knew that my right eye was swollen because I could barely see out of it.

"Stop Lex, that's enough" I heard Jada say. I wasn't surprised that she was here either. Anywhere Alexus went, she was sure to follow. This was one time I was happy that she was here to intervene.

"Alexus, stop! You're going to kill her!" Jada screamed again since Lex didn't listen to her the first time. This time, she had to actually pull her off of me.

"Bitch, you better think twice before you ever try to cross me again!" Alexus yelled before her and Jada disappeared into the night.

I must have had a black cloud following me because my days were getting worse before they got better. I was in so much pain, I couldn't move if I wanted to. The night that I attacked Cherika outside of the store came back to me as I found myself in the same condition that I'd left her in. The only difference was there was no one here to help me when I needed it. Karma was a bitch that I never wanted to meet. Unfortunately, she seemed to have befriended me anyway.

Chapter 8

"Girl, can you please stop crying for every damn thing. It's not the end of the world," Jada fussed as she tried her best to comfort me.

It may not have been the end of the world, but it damn sure felt like it. One of my worst fears had just been confirmed. According to the stick that I'd just peed on, I was pregnant. And if that wasn't bad enough, I had no clue as to who was the father. There was no doubt that it was either Dre or Tyree, but I had no idea which one it was.

"You only took one test, so calm down. These things aren't always one hundred percent accurate. You need to make a doctor's appointment to find out for sure," Jada said.

I was feeling so many emotions right now, but

embarrassment was at the top of the list. I always wondered how women got pregnant and didn't know who the father of their baby was and, now, I was one of them. Even though I took my birth control faithfully, they still weren't one hundred percent effective and I was learning that the hard way. My cycle hadn't come down in about two or three months, but I couldn't go by that. It'd been irregular ever since I started taking my birth control a few years ago.

"I'm going to buy another test and see what it says," I replied.

"Just make a doctor's appointment and find out for sure. That way, they can tell you how far along you are too."

"I don't care how far along I am. I'm not having a damn baby."

"You can't be serious," Jada said, looking at me sideways.

"I'm very serious. First of all, I'll be graduating in a few months and I refuse to be at my graduation with a big ass belly. I also have my clinical training coming up soon. And, most importantly, I don't even know who the damn baby is for." Those were reasons enough for me to do away with this pregnancy as soon as possible.

"You are so fucking selfish. You really need to grow up. You knew what you were doing when you were having unprotected sex with two men at the same time. You made a stupid decision and now you have to pay for it. It's not the baby's fault that things didn't go the way you planned." Jada went off on me and I couldn't even blame her.

"But-" I started talking, but she cut me off.

"But nothing Alexus. Suck that shit up and move on. Everything is not always about you. Even though you and Tyree are not together, you know for a fact that he would take care of his child with no problem. And as much as I hate Dre, I still can't take away the fact that he's a great father. You couldn't ask for two better men as far as this baby is concerned."

That's why I loved my best friend. She didn't hesitate to put me in my place. She made some very good points and I couldn't deny the truth in her words.

"I never thought I'd see the day when you had something good to say about Dre." I laughed but I was serious. If no one else hated Dre, I knew for a fact that Jada did.

"There's a first time for everything. He's still the biggest man whore I know, but he takes damn good care of his kids. I have to give credit where it's due."

"If this is his baby, I'll never get rid of him."

"Well, that's one of the prices that you have to pay. So, are you going to tell them?"

"Hell no! I'm not even one hundred percent sure myself."

"Girl, you're pregnant and I don't need a test to tell me that. You sleep all day and you've been craving seafood for the past few weeks."

"I can't believe my stupid ass was out there fighting while I could possibly be carrying a baby," I said, shaking my head.

A few days ago, I met Keanna outside of her job and gave her the ass whipping of a lifetime. If it wasn't for Jada, I would probably be in jail for murder. I was sick and tired of her always doing something to hurt somebody, so I took all of my anger out on her that night.

"It's not like you knew that you were pregnant at the time. Besides, she needed that beat down in the worse way. Sad part is, it still won't stop her from being messy and ratchet."

"I know it won't, but it felt good beating her ass down."

"Well, let me get this phone book so we can see about making you an appointment as soon as possible," Jada said, walking away.

I was nervous, but at least I had one person in my corner with Jada. I didn't how I was going to tell not one, but two men that I was pregnant and any one of them could be the father. As bad as I wanted to be back with Tyree, I was sure that hearing this news was only going to push him further away from me.

Four days later and I was finally going to see a doctor. I ended up taking two more tests before I came and they all said the same thing, positive. There was no need for me to be in denial any longer. I had to accept my fate. Jada and I walked into the almost empty waiting room and I was in awe. The room was beautifully decorated to resemble an infant's nursery. I couldn't explain it, but I felt a sense of comfort just by being in there.

Dr. Gonzales was a private OBGYN who was deemed as one of the best according to my mother. I ended up telling my mama about the pregnancy not long after I took the first test, and she assured me that everything was going to work out.

I was also thankful to her for keeping me insured. Since I was a college student, I was still considered as one of her dependents. The free clinics in our area were known for keeping you waiting up to four hours before you even saw a doctor. I experienced that with Ayanna when she had her kids and I was happy that I didn't have to go through it.

"Good morning, can I help you?" the friendly receptionist asked when I walked up to her desk. She looked familiar, but I couldn't remember where I'd see her before.

"Yes, I have an appointment with Dr. Gonzales. My name is Alexus Bailey," I said as I signed into the log book.

She stared at me for a minute before looking up my information in the computer.

"Ok, you can have a seat. She'll be out to get you shortly," she replied.

"Why was she staring at you like that?" Jada asked as we sat down.

"I don't know, but I know her from somewhere."

I picked up a magazine that was on the table and flipped through the pages.

"I have something to tell you," Jada said out of the blue. I stopped looking at the book and looked over at her. I hated when she said shit like that because I knew it was going to be something that I didn't want to hear.

"What?" I asked as my heart rate sped up.

Before she had a chance to answer, the door opened and I knew just what she had to tell me. This time, my heart wasn't beating fast; it felt like it had stopped altogether when Tyree walked in.

"No, you didn't," I said through clenched teeth.

"Don't kill me, I'm sorry," she said with a smirk on her face.

I was pissed and I didn't find a damn thing funny. I planned to tell Tyree what was going on, but I wanted to do it when I was ready. Thanks to Tyree's mom, Tyra, intervening, he and Jada were on speaking terms again. He was upset with her because Dre and I got busted in her house. I felt bad about their falling out, so I was extremely happy when they got back on track.

"What's up?" he said as he took a seat next to Jada.

She spoke back, while I pretended to be engrossed in the magazine that I was still holding on to. I felt him looking at me, but I refused to acknowledge his presence.

"Alexus Bailey," I heard coming from the rear of the clinic.

I got up and proceeded in the direction where the doctor's office was located. I expected Jada to get up and follow me, but Tyree came instead. She laughed and shrugged her shoulders when I turned around and looked back at her.

"Hi, I'm Alexus Bailey," I said when I was standing in front of the doctor.

"Nice to meet you, I'm Dr. Gonzales," she said as she shook my hand.

Tyree didn't say anything, but he followed me when she led me to the back and into her office. Once we sat down, I answered the few questions that I was asked before having to taking another pregnancy test. When Dr. Gonzales said she'd be right back, I almost wanted to beg her to stay so I wouldn't have to be left alone with Tyree. I wasn't ready to face my reality.

"So, why did I have to find out that you were pregnant through Jada?" Tyree asked as soon as we were alone.

"I specifically remembered you saying not to call or text you for anything, or did you forget? And you never answered the few times I did try to call anyway."

"That's bullshit and you know it. For something this important, you know I would have wanted to know."

"Well, now you know. It doesn't matter who told you."

"I'm sure you don't know, but I'm gonna ask anyway. Which one of us is the father?" I knew that was coming sooner or later, but he was right; I didn't know who the father was.

"You're right; I don't know, but a simple blood test will solve the mystery once the baby gets here," I said with an attitude.

"I don't want to have to wait until the baby is born to find out if it's mine. I can't go through all these months of guessing."

"Well, how else are you going to find out? As a matter of fact, why are you even here? You could have stayed in the waiting room, just like Jada did."

Dr. Gonzales came back into the room before he had a chance to answer and I was more than happy when she did.

"Ok, so you are definitely pregnant," she said as if I didn't know that already. "I want to do an ultrasound so we can see just how far along you are."

"Can I ask you a question?" Tyree asked her.

"Sure, you can," she replied with a smile.

"Can we get a paternity test done before the baby is born?"

Dr. Gonzales looked uncomfortable for a minute, but she quickly regained her composure and answered his question. I, on the other hand, was too embarrassed to even look at her.

"Um, yes you can, but I really don't recommend it. The procedure is called amniocentesis and it does pose a slight risk of miscarriage, which is why I don't suggest doing it. Once the baby is born, you can get an expedited DNA test done and the results come back within 24 hours."

"Ok, thanks," he replied, seemingly satisfied with the answer he received.

After taking a sonogram, I found out that I was eight weeks pregnant. Tyree seemed more interested in what was going on than I did, but he tried to play it off. I didn't ask the doctor any questions, but he had a million. After she answered so many, she finally gave him a bunch of pamphlets to read.

"Ok, I'll see you back in about four weeks. Make sure you schedule your next appointment with the receptionist," Dr. Gonzales said as she saw us out.

Jada was still sitting in the waiting room when we came out. She was asking me questions about what the doctor said, but I didn't get a chance to answer her. Tyree took over and told her everything that took place from the minute we got into the room. He even told her what the doctor said about the paternity test. I didn't know if it was my hormones kicking in or what, but I was ready to get away from his ass. I walked up to the receptionist desk to make an appointment for next month with Tyree and Jada close behind.

"What's up T.J.?" the receptionist asked, speaking to Tyree.

"What's up with you? I haven't seen too much of you since you left the nursing home," he replied.

I looked at her name tag and everything was starting to come back to me. Kelly was a nurse that Keanna worked with at the nursing home. I saw her there a few times when I went to visit Tyree. She was always so loud and common. She was also very messy, so I knew for a fact that she was going to call Keanna as soon as we left. Dre was going to find out about this pregnancy whether I wanted him to or not. I just had to be prepared for it when he did.

Chapter 9

I didn't know why the fuck Keanna was blowing my phone up, but she was wasting her time calling me. I was done entertaining her and all the drama that she came with. I was on my way to pick up my pops and my brother, Eric, and chill with them for a while. I had a lot on my mind and I needed somebody to talk to. I'd been making a lot of stupid decisions lately and I needed advice from somebody who would give it to me straight. Whether I was right or wrong, those were the two that would give it to me raw and uncut, and they didn't care if I got mad about it. I wasn't going to have my kids until later today, so we decided to go to Hooters for some food and drinks.

"What's up?" Eric spoke as he hopped into the back seat of my truck. "Man, Keanna's been blowing my phone up looking for you."

"Man, fuck Keanna!" I yelled as I waved him off.

"She told me that her and ole girl had a fight the other day." He got my undivided attention when he said that.

"Who did she have a fight with?" I had a feeling that I already knew but I asked anyway.

"Alexus," he replied, confirming what I assumed.

"What the hell were they fighting for?" I knew it was because of what Keanna and I had done, but I wanted to see what she told him.

"I don't know. She just said that they had a fight outside of the club where she works."

"Well I already know that Lex beat that ass. They can't hang with her when it comes to fighting."

"She didn't tell me all that, but she did say that she had to talk to you about something important."

We pulled up to our fathers' house so I didn't reply to what he'd just said.

"Boy, call Keanna and see what the hell she wants," my pops said when he entered the truck. "She's getting on my damn nerves."

"Damn, she's calling you too?" I asked him as I pulled off.

"I don't know why you don't answer your phone and talk to her yourself." He sounded aggravated so I'm sure she called more times than she actually needed to.

"I'll call her back later," I lied. I didn't have any intentions on calling her back anytime soon. Keanna was one member of my family that I could do without.

Ten minutes later, we were being seated at the fairly empty restaurant. It was the middle of the day, so the crowd was light. Our half-dressed waitress took our food and drink orders as soon as we sat down.

"So, what's going on with you and Cherika? You better stop playing with that girl's feelings. If you don't want her no more, leave her alone." My pops wasn't a big fan of Cherika's but he tolerated her because of the kids.

"Nothing's going on with us. She knows that we're not together."

"But you keep sleeping with her. You're sending her mixed messages. You can handle sex with no strings attached, but she can't. And then you went out there and got another crazy one on your hands," he said, shaking his head.

He was referring to Mya, a chick that I met when I was in the rehabilitation center a few months ago. She worked there as a receptionist and we starting kicking it not long after I got there. She was on some bullshit about us being in a relationship lately, but I wasn't feeling it. When I told her about my situation with Cherika and Alexus, she seemed to be cool with it. Now, she was one step away from being a stalker. She either called me day and night, or she wanted to be with me all the time.

Then, to make matters worse, I started sleeping with Cherika again and she was back on that marriage counseling shit. She held out on me for a while but, when I told her that I wanted to try and work things out, she was all in. At the time, I really felt like I wanted to try again, but I'm still not ready just yet. In the back of my mind, I was still holding out hope that Alexus and I would work things out eventually. I would hate to get back with Cherika only to put her through the same thing again.

"He wants Alexus. That's why he's not trying to get serious with nobody else," Eric said, almost reading my mind.

"And you need to leave her alone too. She seems to be just as confused as you are," my pops noted.

The waitress came back with our drinks before I had a chance to respond. Right after I took the first sip of my beer, my phone started ringing. It was no surprise that it was Keanna once again. As much as I didn't want to answer, curiosity was getting the best of me and I just had to see what she wanted.

"What Keanna," I barked when I answered the phone.

"Where are you? We need to talk," she answered.

"Don't worry about where I am, just start talking. It better be important, the way you've been blowing up everybody's phone."

"When's the last time you talked to Alexus?"

"Why? I already know that she whipped your ass if that's what you're calling to tell me."

"Whatever, but that's not why I'm calling."

"Ok, so what do you want?" I was getting impatient with her stalling.

"Did you know that she's pregnant?"

I swear, the world stopped spinning when she said that. I hadn't talked to Alexus since everything went down at Jada's house a while ago, but, if she was pregnant, she had a lot of explaining to do. The first thing I had to do was find out if what Keanna said was true.

"Who told you that?"

"My friend, Kelly, works at the doctor's office. She told me that Alexus and Tyree were in there yesterday and she's like two months pregnant."

I was speechless to say the least. If Alexus was two months pregnant, there was a very strong possibility that the baby could be mine. Then, to hear Keanna say that ole boy was at the clinic with her pissed me off to no end. I just hope they didn't think that they were going to live happily ever after with a child that I was the father of. They had me fucked all the way up if they did.

"Alright Keanna, I'll talk to you later," I said, hanging up the phone. The waitress came back with our food, but my appetite was gone. I needed to talk to Alexus to see what was going on. Without a blood test, there was no way for her to convince me that she wasn't carrying my child.

"What did she want?" Eric asked me. He and my pops were looking at me, waiting for my answer. It didn't make sense to lie. Knowing Keanna, my entire family would know about it before the end of the day.

"She said that Alexus is pregnant," I replied, lowering my head.

"Awe, shit! You better get yourself together boy. You got a crazy ass wife, another crazy ass girlfriend and now you then got somebody else pregnant." My pops was fussing at me like I wasn't a grown ass man.

"Wait," Eric said, holding up his hand. "I thought she was dealing with somebody else. You don't know for sure if that's your baby or not."

"Nah, but I'm damn sure gon' find out," I replied. Alexus already knew that I was not that nigga to be played with. Since she still had my number blocked, I was going to pay her a visit. I didn't know where she was staying, but that wouldn't be too hard to find out. Getting at Alexus was only one of the many problems that I would have to deal with. When Cherika found out, that was going to be a real disaster.

After dropping my pops and brother off home, I made my way over to Jada's house. If anybody knew how to get in touch with Alexus, Jada was that person. I parked my car in front and made my way to her front door. After ringing her doorbell three times, I started pounding on her screen door. I knew that she was there because her car was parked in the driveway.

"Why the hell are you knocking on my door like you're the police?" she yelled when she snatched the door open.

"Where's Alexus?" I asked, getting right to the point.

"She's not here, but I'm sure you're probably the last person that she wants to talk to anyway."

"Do you know where's she's at?" I ignored her smart-ass remark because I wasn't in the mood.

"No, I don't. You need to just leave her alone and go on about your business. You've already done enough damage."

I wasn't trying to go back and forth with her about something that didn't concern her, but I said what was on my mind anyway.

"I'll be happy to go on about my business as soon as I find out if she's carrying my baby or not," I replied as I turned to walk away.

I was sure that she was wondering how I found out as I left her standing there with a blank expression on her face. I hopped in my truck and prepared to make my way over to Alexus' mom's house when my phone started ringing. It didn't surprise me when I saw Mya's number pop up on my screen. I pressed the ignore button and continued on my way. I had to ignore five more calls before she eventually gave up and stopped calling. Mya was cool to chill with, but she was almost as bad as Cherika and she wasn't even my wife.

When I pulled up to Alexus' mom's house, I got happy when I saw her car in the driveway. I hadn't seen her in a while, so just the thought alone made me smile inside. I parked my car and was about to get out, until my phone started ringing again. This time, it was Cherika, so I decided to answer and see what she wanted.

"Yeah!" I said, yelling into the receiver. As soon as she started talking, I regretted answering the phone at all.

76

"So, is it true?" she asked, crying into the phone.

"Is what true?" I played dumb even though I already knew what she was talking about. That damn Keanna was never going to change. She and Cherika didn't even speak, so I wondered how she was able to deliver the news to her so fast.

"Please don't play dumb with me, Dre. You know exactly what I'm talking about. Keanna told your mama and your sisters that Alexus is pregnant. I just want to hear it from you if the baby is yours or not." Well, at least I knew exactly how she found out.

"It probably is, but I don't know for sure." I was being honest but I'm sure that didn't matter to her.

"Oh, my God. I can't believe this," Cherika said in between sobs. This was the shit that I hated about her. She always begged me for the truth, but she couldn't take it when I gave it to her.

"Let me call you right back Cherika."

I didn't even give her a chance to reply before I hung up. I wasn't in the mood for all that crying and shit. I already had enough to deal with.

I got out of my car and walked up to the front door. Before I had a chance to knock, the door swung open and I was face to face with Anita, Alexus' mom.

"How you doing Ms. Anita? Is Alexus here?" I asked in my most pleasant voice.

With a frown on her face, she looked me up and down before she went back into the house and closed the door in my face. I was about to ring the doorbell until I heard her rude ass yelling for her daughter to come downstairs.

"You can wait out here, she's coming," Ms. Anita said as she came back outside.

I shook my head and laughed to myself. She was making it known that I wasn't welcomed into her house. That was all good for now but, if this baby turned out to be mine,

77

she would be seeing a lot more of me whether she wanted to or not. She got in her car and pulled off just as Alexus made it to the door.

"What are you doing here Dre?" Alexus asked with a disgusted look on her face.

When I looked at her, it felt like I was falling in love all over again. She had her long hair pulled back into a ponytail, displaying the beautiful features that made up her face. I looked down at her stomach, but nothing was different. It was still as flat as it was the last time I saw her.

"Don't you think we need to talk?" I asked after staring at her for a while.

"No, we don't have anything to talk about." She turned to walk away but I grabbed her arm.

"So, when were you planning to tell me that you're pregnant?" I asked, stopping her in her tracks. She turned around and looked at me, but she didn't seem surprised that I knew.

"I was going to tell you, but I kind of figured that somebody was going to beat me to it."

"So, whose baby is it?"

"No way for me to know that until a blood test is done."

"When's the next time you go to the doctor?"

"I don't know."

"Do you need anything?"

"Not from you, I don't. Thanks, but you've already done enough." Her voice was dripping with sarcasm but that was nothing new.

"What do you mean by that?"

"Don't play stupid with me, Dre. I know exactly what you did, but I'm not even mad at you. I put myself in that situation, so I take full blame for what happened. That was a much-needed learning experience for me and I've definitely learned my lesson. I lost someone that I was in love with behind another woman's husband and it wasn't even worth it."

It hurt me to hear her say that she was in love with someone else. More than that, it hurt me to know that it was really over between us. I'd never heard her talk with so much conviction in her voice, so I knew that she meant exactly what she said. Being with me was a mistake that she didn't want to make again.

"You know I'm always going to love you, right?"

"That's the problem Dre. You have a wife. You shouldn't even be standing here professing your love to another woman."

"It's not like I'm lying. I can't help how I feel about you. It is what it is."

"Well, it's not a good idea for us to talk or see each other. I'll text to keep you updated about the baby. I don't need you to come to the doctor with me, but we'll do a blood test as soon as it comes," she said, pissing me off.

"So, it's cool for your man to come to your appointments, but I can't? Me and that nigga are rocking in the same boat as far as this baby goes. It's a possibility that either one of us is the father."

"Honestly, I don't need nobody to come with me. I made my bed and I'm prepared to lay in it alone."

"You know that will never happen as long as I'm around," I said as I reached out and touched her face. She backed away from me like my touch was poisonous.

"I've been doing a lot of thinking and I came to a conclusion. If you didn't have anybody who was willing to cheat with you, you wouldn't have cheated. I made it easy for you to do what you were doing and it cost me in the end. Tyree didn't deserve it and neither did your wife."

"Why are you trying to make it seem like being with me was so bad?" I was getting frustrated with her trying to put me down. I never claimed to be perfect and she knew what was up with me.

"I'm not saying that it was bad. I'm saying that it shouldn't have happened."

I'd never felt so defeated in my life. I admit that I went about doing things the wrong way, but my intentions were always good. No matter which way I turned, somebody was going to end up hurt in the end. And as selfish as it might have sounded, I didn't want that someone to be me.

"Can you at least unblock my number so I can check on you sometimes?"

"No, Dre. I'll text you after every appointment, just to keep you informed."

"What! That's only once a month!" I yelled. She was really trying to make me go there.

"Well, what else do you want? I only see the doctor once a month."

"I'm trying to handle this the right way, but you're really starting to piss me off. If you don't want to be with me no more, then that's cool, but you got me fucked up if you think I'm letting you call all the shots when my baby is involved. Now, either we come up with some kind of agreement or I'll invite myself to all of your appointments and everywhere else that you go."

She pulled her phone out of her pocket and scrolled through the contacts until she came to my name. She turned the phone around so that I could see that my number had been unblocked.

"The first time you call me about something other than this baby, you're going on block indefinitely."

"Do you need some money or something?"

"No, I'm fine. I'm gotta finish studying so I'll talk to you some other time," she said as she turned to go inside. I didn't get the results I wanted, but at least I made some progress. I watched her walk away, like always, and the view was still perfect.

Chapter 10

I didn't know how much more I was expected to endure from my husband, but I was at my breaking point. Once again, I'd fallen for his lies and bullshit. And as usual, I was having regrets. He swore that he wanted to move on and make our marriage work, but his actions weren't matching his words. He was acting like it was no big deal that he'd possibly gotten another woman pregnant. Dre admitted that there was a possibility that Alexus' baby could be his. I was crushed, to say the least. I not only took pride in being Dre's wife, but I was also happy knowing that I was the only woman to ever bear his children. Now, it seemed like all of that was about to change.

Then, I found out from his sisters that he had somebody else in the picture. Mya was the chick that worked at the rehabilitation center that Dre was in a few months ago. I had a feeling that something was going on with them the first time I saw her. She gave me a strange look when I introduced myself as Dre's wife when I visited him there. It was also something about the way they looked at each other that just didn't sit too well with me.

I thought back to what Dr. Reynolds, the marriage counselor that we saw, told me a little while ago. She said that even if Alexus was out of the picture, how could I be sure that there wouldn't be someone else. I never thought about it that way, but she was absolutely right. I just assumed that, if there was no Alexus, we would be fine. The truth was, with Dre, there would always be someone else.

I felt myself slipping back into my old ways and it was hard to stop it. I hadn't gone to church in two weeks and that wasn't helping my situation either. But, I did pay attention to one thing in particular. Not one time did Dre's family, nor my kids, mention Alexus being around lately. Erica told me that he came over once with another girl, whom I assumed was Mya, but she stayed outside in the car. According to her, Alexus hadn't been around in a while. Even when I asked my kids, I got the same answer. They hadn't seen her around lately either. Maybe she really was done with him this time around. It was a little too late since she was already pregnant, but she was one less problem for me to worry about.

"Can we bring our PlayStation over to our daddy's house mama?" Lil Dre asked when he entered the kitchen.

"Yeah, but make sure you bring a game that all of you can play," I responded.

My kids were waiting for Dre to pick them up and so was I. I needed some time to myself. My mama's church was having a revival tonight, but I really didn't feel like going, even though I needed to. Although I never answered the phone, she'd been calling me non-stop since this morning, begging me to attend. I made the mistake of telling her everything that went down between Dre and I. I even told her about Alexus being pregnant. I knew that it was a stupid move, but I really needed a shoulder to cry on and she was the only one I had at the time.

The ringing of my doorbell temporarily pulled me away from my troubles. I was washing dishes so I couldn't answer it at the moment.

"Lil Dre, open the door for your daddy!" I yelled to my son.

I was happy that it was daytime and my kids were awake. If not, Dre would have been trying to get me to have sex with him again and I really was not feeling it. I'd made up my mind to stop having sex with him altogether. Being intimate with Dre seemed to further complicate things for me. I loved my husband entirely too much to just have a casual fling with him. I wanted all or nothing. If he couldn't give me all of him, I wasn't taking scraps. I'd done that long enough and I was tired. It just seemed like walking away was the hardest part because I didn't know how. I'd always had issues with my self-esteem and going on this roller coaster ride with Dre wasn't helping.

After a few minutes of hearing nothing, I dried my hands and went into the living room. Lil Dre was still standing at the partially opened door, but I didn't see his daddy anywhere.

"Why are you just standing there?"

My son was looking at crazy as I approached the door to see what was up. I pulled it all the way open and I immediately regretted my decision to do so.

"What the hell are you doing here?" I asked as I looked up into Troy's smiling face.

"I heard that you have something here that belongs to me," he said, walking into my house uninvited.

My kids ran downstairs with their bags, probably thinking that our unwanted visitor was their father.

"I don't have a damn thing here that belongs to you, so get the fuck out!"

"Come here lil man." Troy reached his arms out for Drew to come to him.

Drew was very shy, so there was no way he was going to go to a stranger. And that's exactly what Troy was to him. He ran over to me and wrapped his tiny arms around my legs.

"Get out Troy!" I needed him to be long gone before Dre got here. Things were already bad between us but, if he caught Troy here, they would only get worse.

"Come here and say hello to your daddy." He continued talking to Drew while completely ignoring me.

"You are not his daddy."

"Well, that's not what the blood test said." He walked over to me but I refused to back down.

"Get out before I call the police to escort you out," I said nervously.

"Bitch, I'm not walking out that door until I'm good and ready," he replied arrogantly.

"Nah, nigga, you not gon' walk out; you gon' get carried out," Dre said as he and Eric walked through the front door.

All the color drained from Troy's face as Dre rushed him with a barrage of powerful blows to his face and body. Eric pulled me and my kids into the kitchen as they completely destroyed my living room. As long as I'd known Dre, I'd never seem him this angry before. He was throwing Troy around my living room like he weighed nothing at all.

"Dre stop, please," I cried as I saw the wreck that was once considered my front room.

"Shut up and let him handle his business. That nigga deserve to get his ass beat," Eric said as he stood by and watched Dre beat Troy into a pulp.

I thought for sure that he would intervene when he saw his brother stomping his used to be best friend, but he did nothing to stop it. Troy was trying his best to defend himself, but it was useless. His face, along with my carpet, was a bloody mess. My children were crying and screaming as they watched their father viciously beat another man right before their eyes. When Dre looked up and saw them, it was only then that he decided to stop his brutal attack.

"Go put my kids in the car!" he breathlessly yelled to his brother. Eric picked Drew up and instructed the rest of the kids to follow him out of the house and into Dre's awaiting truck. I panicked when I saw Dre walk back over to where Troy was, so I jumped in front of him to stop him from starting up again.

"Get the fuck out of the way! It's your fault that all of this shit happened in the first place!" he yelled at me. True to his word, I cleared a path for him as he dragged a semi unconscious Troy by his collar and literally threw him out of the house.

"He just showed up here. I didn't know that he was going to come." I followed behind him, trying to explain myself.

It was of no use. Completely ignoring me, he hopped in his truck and burned rubber as he sped off. Troy had managed to pull himself up into a sitting position, but I didn't stay outside long enough to see what he was about to do. I couldn't believe that Dre had left him here on my lawn knowing that I was home by myself.

As soon as I got inside, I grabbed the phone and called the police. I wasn't taking any chances with Troy. I told the operator what was going on and she assured me that a car was on the way. The next call I made was to my mother. I said that I wasn't going to church with her tonight, but I quickly changed my mind after today's events. Plus, I wanted to spend a few nights at her house so I wouldn't be in here alone for the next few days. I packed a bag and sat in my room and waited for the police to show up.

Later that evening, I sat in my mother's spare bedroom and prepared to get ready for the church service that we were about to attend. I felt so much better now that I was away from my house and all the madness that took place earlier. It took about thirty minutes for the police to show up and Troy had already left by the time they arrived. I did have a police report on file just in case anything else happened after that. I tried calling Dre again to explain what happened, but he never came to the phone. Whenever I called, he would let one of our children answer. It's like he was trying to punish me for something that I didn't do.

"Are you ready to go?" my sister, Cherice, asked as she entered the room. My mama had managed to get all of us to come to her church's revival tonight and she was very happy about it. We hadn't all gone to church together since we were kids.

"I guess so," I said sadly.

"What's wrong?" She came and stood in front of me, waiting for me to answer her question.

"Everything is wrong. Dre is mad with me because of what happened earlier with Troy. I swear, I didn't know that he was going to show up over there. I don't even know what made him come in the first place." I was tired of crying but that didn't stop the tears from falling.

"Stop crying. You didn't do anything wrong. Why do you let Dre control your emotions like that?"

"I'm trying not to, but it's hard. Every time I feel like I'm getting over him, he comes right back and makes me fall in love all over again. It's like he only wants me when I don't want him."

"He knows exactly what he's doing. All of this is a game to him. He's knows that all he has to do is say what you want to hear and you'll take him back. You make it too easy. You have to say no and mean no."

"You make it sound so easy, but it's not. I just don't know what I'm doing wrong. I'm doing everything that I can to show him that I've changed. I really feel like I'm losing my mind sometimes."

"Let's go. It sounds like you need church more than any of us." Cherice grabbed my hand and pulled me out of the room.

We were a little late getting to church, but my mother's friend saved us a seat right up front. My sisters were having a fit but, since I'd been coming here for the past few weeks, I'd gotten used to it. My mother had to be up front or it just wasn't right.

I couldn't explain it, but calmness came over me every time I stepped into the sanctuary. Whatever problems I was having at the time didn't seem so bad when I was here.

After three hours, church was still going strong and they didn't seem like they would be ending anytime soon. Baptist churches could go on for days if they thought the members would stay that long. I tried to hold out as long as I could, but my bladder was winning the battle that I tried hard to fight.

"Come with me to the bathroom. I feel like I'm about to bust," I whispered to my sister, Cherice.

"Girl, me too; let's go," she whispered back. When we stood up, Charde jumped up too without even bothering to ask where we were going. We excused ourselves from the pew and made our way through the back of the church to the bathrooms. As soon as we walked into the bathroom, Cherice and I made a beeline for the empty stalls while Charde played with her hair in the huge wall mirror. When we were done, we stood at the sink and washed our hands.

"What time is this going to be over with?" Charde asked, sounding annoyed.

"I don't know, but I hope it's soon. Let's go before mama comes back here looking for us," I said as I headed for the bathroom's exit.

Just as I was pushing the door to go out, someone was pulling the handle to come in. As soon as the door opened, I was at a loss for words when I locked eyes with Alexus.

Chapter 11

I couldn't believe it. Church was the one place that was supposed to be drama free, but here I was standing face to face with Cherika and her sisters. Tyree's grandmother was a member of the church and she invited Tyra and the twins to their revival service tonight. Since I was spending the night at their house, they invited me to come along with them. With all that I'd been through within the past few months, I gladly accepted the invitation.

Although the place was full of people, I never expected Cherika to be one of them. We looked at each other, but no words were spoken as I walked pass them and entered the stall. I was almost four months pregnant and this baby lived on my bladder. When I was done emptying my full bladder, I washed my hands and made my exit. I was both shocked and disgusted to see that Cherika and her sisters were waiting for me in the empty hallway. I knew they were hood, but I hoped they weren't trying to pop off in the church of all places. I wasn't scared, so I walked right past them and prepared to retake my seat.

"Alexus, can I talk to you for a minute?" Cherika asked in a civilized tone. I was tempted to walk away, but she didn't sound like she was on no bullshit, so I stopped and turned around to face her.

"Talk to me about what? If it's about Dre, then there's nothing to discuss. That's over and done with."

She looked down at the small pouch that was forming in front of me before she started talking again.

"Well, he told me that our kids are going to have a little brother or sister soon." She kept her eyes focused on my stomach as she spoke.

"No disrespect to your kids, but I hope not. I'm trying to get myself together and I really don't want to have anything to do with Dre."

"He must have cheated on you too," her sister, Charde, said sarcastically. I had to remember where I was. Other than that, I would have had a few choice words for her nasty ass.

"What happened between y'all, if you don't mind me asking?" Cherice questioned.

She seemed to be the more sensible one out of the three of them. Even though she seemed cool, I didn't know or trust her enough to tell her my business.

"Nothing really happened between us. I just don't want to be with him no more," was my simple, but honest reply.

"So, that's why he's trying so hard to make things work with you all of a sudden." Cherice looked at Cherika like they had finally solved a mystery. That revelation didn't surprise me at all. Dre was a user and a manipulator. He would be the perfect husband until somebody else came along to occupy his time.

92

"He's just gonna find somebody else to cheat with," Charde said. She seemed to enjoy rubbing salt in her sister's wounds. Cherika was giving her the look of death and she quickly got the message and closed her mouth.

"I don't know about all of that, but I can promise you that I won't be the one that he's cheating with. Experience is the best teacher and I've learned my lesson. I'm just sorry that it took me so long to get it right," I noted.

It took me losing Tyree to see that being with Dre was not worth it. I didn't want to end up losing myself like Cherika did. If God saw fit to send me another good man in the future, I was going to do everything in my power to do right by him.

"So, what if that's his baby? You know how Dre feels about his children. He's not just gonna go away because you want him to," Cherika said.

It felt weird having a normal conversation with her. Usually when we saw each other, we were either fussing or fighting. She seemed to have matured over the last few months. Maybe it was because she was attending church now.

"If this is his baby, I'm not trying to keep him away from it. But, at the same time, I don't have to be with him just because we have a child together. Honestly, I haven't even thought that far ahead because I pray that it's not his."

"Well, that makes two of us."

I should have been offended by what she said, but I wasn't. I understood how she felt. She was his wife so, of course, she didn't want his ex-side chick to have his baby.

"Well, good luck to you with everything," Cherice said.

"Thanks," I replied before I walked away.

I could feel them staring at me as I left, but I really didn't care. We had both said what we had to say and the conversation was over. I walked down the aisle and returned to my seat next to Tyra.

Later that night, the twins and I were lounging around in the living room watching tv. We ended up leaving the church service early because it didn't seem like it was ever going to end. After taking my shower, I threw on my pajamas and prepared to pig out on the bag of junk food that Tyra bought for me. I was always so lazy when I came over here because they waited on me hand and foot. They even picked me up from my mama's house so I didn't have to drive if I didn't want to. Even though they knew that Tyree might not be my baby's father, they still treated me the same. They even assured me that they would help me with him or her whenever they were born. Besides my mama, that was about the only help that I would have. Dre's family hated me so I knew that I couldn't depend on them for anything, not that I wanted to.

"So, what are we watching tonight?" Trina asked, sitting down next to me.

Tina read through a list of movies until we all decided on which one to watch. They always gave me control of the remote so that I could pause the movie whenever I needed to. I ran to the bathroom a lot, so I had to use it almost every half hour.

"Tee said that he's grilling you some seafood tomorrow pretty girl," Tyra said when she walked into the living room.

Mr. Tee was her husband and Tyree's father. Since I'd been pregnant, seafood was what I craved the most and Mr. Tee kept me fully supplied whenever I came over.

"Put the movie on," Tyra said as she sat down.

She always started out watching the movies with us, but she would always leave and go to her room before it ended. I loved the way Tyree's parents got along. They'd been married for over twenty years, but they still acted like newlyweds. Whenever her husband was ready to go to bed, she would leave us and retire to her room for the night.

An hour and two bathroom breaks later, we were all lounging comfortably around the living room watching tv, when the rattle of keys could be heard at the front door.

"That must be TJ," Tyra said as the key was inserted into the lock.

My heart immediately dropped at the mention of his name. Besides my doctors' appointments and a few texts messages to see how I was doing; Tyree and I didn't have a lot of contact with each other. When he said that he was done with me, he meant exactly what he said. I smiled when he opened the door and walked in. My smile quickly faded when I saw Kayla walk in behind him. I had no right to be, but I was hurt. He didn't waste any time moving on. And the fact that he'd moved on with Kayla made me suspect that something might have been going on all along.

"Good evening everybody," she said when she walked in. Nobody spoke back and I think it was because we were all shocked to see her there.

"Where's my pops?" Tyree asked, not bothering to speak to any of us. He looked just as uncomfortable as everyone else did, but at least he could have said hello.

"He's in his office," Tyra replied.

Walking in the direction of his father's office, Tyree left Kayla standing in the living room with us. After a few uncomfortable seconds, she walked off as well, going in the same direction that he went in.

"Uh, you can have a seat. He'll be right back." Tyra stopped her in her tracks before she got a chance to go too far.

"Oh, ok," was her nervous reply as she occupied a spot on the loveseat. Tyra got up and headed to the back with a look on her face that told me that she was not happy. The twins and

I continued watching the movie while ignoring the unwanted presence in the room.

"So, how many months are you?" Kayla asked when she saw me rubbing my slightly protruding belly.

"None of your damn business!" Trina snapped before I had a chance to respond.

Tina and I looked at her like she was crazy for making the unwarranted outburst. In all honesty, I felt bad for Kayla because I knew exactly how she felt. Dre's family treated me like shit because Cherika was who they liked. It wasn't her fault that they wanted me and Tyree to be together. I was the one who messed that up.

"I'll be four months next week," I replied nicely.

I was hoping to soften the blow just a little. Before she had a chance to say anything else, we heard raised voices coming from the back of the house. I couldn't make out what they were saying, but I could definitely tell that it was Tyree and his parents arguing. Once the shouting match ended, Tyree came storming from the back like a mad man.

"Let's go," he said to Kayla as he hurried past us and out the front door. Tyra was right on his heels and followed him onto the porch.

"You better be here tomorrow, just like I said!" she yelled at him.

I didn't hear him reply, but I did hear when his tires screeched as he pulled off. When Tyra came back in, she went straight to the back of the house without saying anything.

" Are you alright Lex?" Tina asked, grabbing my hand.

"Yeah, I'm good," I lied. I actually felt like crying, but that wouldn't change anything. As much as it pained me to do so, I had to lie in the bed in which I'd made for myself.

Chapter 12

The ringing of my phone jolted me from a much-needed sound sleep. According to the clock that rested on the wall, it was almost eleven in the morning, which only gave me another hour until it was time to check out. I'd spent yet another night holed up in a hotel with Kayla. I lost count of the many times she begged me to come to her house, but I always refused. And there was no way in hell that she was ever coming to mine. I wasn't trying to lead her on and make her think that what we were doing was nothing more than sex because that's all it was. As long as we were on the same page, it was cool.

I made sure that I was honest up front. That way, she had a choice of whether she wanted to stay or go. It didn't matter to me one way or the other because I already had enough on my plate. My family was problem number one.

They were pissed about me bringing Kayla to their house last night. My intentions were to pick her up and go straight to the hotel, but a call from my father changed my plans. He needed me to sign some papers that had to be faxed right away, so I really didn't have a choice. I didn't know that Alexus was there or I would have left Kayla in the car. Even though she did me wrong, I still loved her and I was still in love with her. Stressing her out was the last thing that I wanted to do, especially since she was pregnant.

And that was another thing that was bothering me. I was really torn when it came down to this whole pregnancy thing. As much as I wanted to say "fuck it" and move on, I just couldn't do it. The fact remained that there was a possibility that I could be the father, just as well as her ex. That was the main reason why I made sure to be at every doctor's appointment. If I was the father, at least I could say that I was there every step of the way. But, on the flip side, it was going to kill me if I'd been there all along, only to find out that the baby was for someone else.

"Yeah Ma," I said, answering my phone. This was the fourth time she called this morning, so I knew she was pissed.

"Don't 'yeah ma' me. Did you forget that I told you I wanted to talk to you today?"

"No, I didn't forget. You never gave me a time."

"Well, the sooner the better."

"Alright, let me take a shower and eat. I'll be there when I'm done."

"I cooked and your daddy is grilling, so you can eat when you get here."

"Cool, I'll see you in a little while," I replied before disconnecting our call.

I sat up and swung my legs to the side of the bed. I never brought changing clothes when we stayed at the hotel, so I needed to go home and change.

"I hope you're not trying to leave without me," Kayla said as she sat up in the bed. Her timing was perfect because I was ready to bounce.

"Nah, but I need to be somewhere. Get dressed, so I can bring you to your car."

Kayla and I never came to each other's houses. We always met up at a neutral spot. She would park her car somewhere safe and ride with me. That was my suggestion and it was working out pretty good thus far.

"Are we hooking up again tonight?"

Every time we were about to go our separate ways, she always wanted to know how long it would be before she saw me again. And, every time, I gave her the same answer.

"I don't know. We'll see how our day goes," was my generic answer.

"Can I ask you something?"

"What's up?"

"I know that you have a lot on your plate right now, but I need to know about us. What are we doing? I mean, do you even see us having a future together?" She was rambling on, even though I raised my hand to stop her from talking.

"From day one, I was straight up and honest with you. I'm not looking for anything serious. I just got out of a serious relationship that didn't end too well."

"You still love her, don't you?" Her voice was low, almost like she was afraid to ask.

"Yes, and I've told you that several times."

"Even after everything that she's done to you. You caught her cheating or did you forget?"

This was the reason why I never told anyone my business. I hated for someone to throw something I'd told them back in my face. That was my fault though. I was hurt but I cried on the wrong shoulder.

"Not that it's any of your business, but I can't turn my feelings off like that. I can't love somebody one day and stop the next. That's not how it works."

"You're gonna be stupid and go right back to her," she said, just above a whisper. If the room wasn't so quiet, I probably would have missed it. I noticed that she'd been in her feelings a lot lately and it was time for me to put her in her place.

"I can see that you don't know how to fuck without catching feelings, so this here is a wrap," I said, standing to my feet.

"I'm just afraid of being hurt in the long run if you end up getting back with her."

"You don't have to worry about that happening. Like I just said, it's a wrap. I have enough to deal with without worrying about all the added drama."

I grabbed my clothes that were scattered on the floor and proceeded to get dressed. Kayla grabbed her things and stormed off to the bathroom and slammed the door. I had a feeling that this was going to happen, but I was putting a stop to it before it got out of hand.

After dropping Kayla off to her car, I went home and took a shower, before getting dressed to go talk to my mother. It was crazy for me to feel this way, but I was hoping that Alexus was still there. She should have been the last person on my mind, but she wasn't. I pulled into my parents' driveway, but I didn't see Lex's car there. That didn't mean anything because I didn't see her car last night either, but she was still there. Since my pops was grilling, I decided to enter through the yard instead of the front door. When I entered the yard, I saw my sisters and Jada sitting at the table playing cards. My pops was on the grill, but I didn't see my mama or Alexus anywhere.

"What's up y'all?" I greeted everyone as I made my way into the house. I walked into the kitchen and found my mama standing at the stove cooking.

"I see you finally made it," she said when I leaned over to kiss her cheek.

"I told you that I was coming," I replied.

I wanted to ask her where Alexus was since I still hadn't seen her. Before I had a chance to ask, she came strolling into the kitchen with the phone up to her ear. She looked so cute in a colorful sundress that put her tiny baby bump on full display. She was always pretty, but the pregnancy gave her a glow that she didn't have before.

"Is the food done?" she asked my mama, completely ignoring me.

"In about ten minutes, it will be," my mama replied, smiling.

I felt some kind of way about her acting like I wasn't in the room. Then, she was on the phone laughing with somebody and that made me just as mad. My sisters kept telling me that she wasn't dealing with her ex anymore, but that was the only person I could think of that would have her smiling so hard. I no longer had the right to question her, but I really wanted to know who she was talking to. I was happy that I didn't have to wonder for long because my suspicions were quickly put to rest.

"Tyra, my mama said hi and send her a plate," Alexus said as she laughed along with my mama.

They went back and forth for a little while before she finally disconnected the call. Even after getting off the phone, it still seemed as if I was invisible to her as she continued talking to my mama like I wasn't even in the room.

"Well damn, hello to you too, Alexus," I said after feeling like I'd been ignored long enough.

"Oh, so now you see me. You sure didn't seem to see me last night. Keep that same energy." She walked outside before I even had a chance to reply.

"That must be those damn pregnancy hormones getting to her."

"That has nothing to do with her attitude. She's right. You came in here last night and didn't bother to acknowledge any of us."

At first, I was getting mad about her jumping to Alexus' defense. I didn't pay much attention to it until she brought it up, but she was right. It wasn't intentional but I didn't speak to anyone when I walked in the house the night before.

"So, what's going on with y'all?" She caught me off guard with the question, but I had no problem giving her the answer.

"Nothing is going on with us. She cheated and I'm done with her. She can do her and I'll do me."

"I hope you're not talking about doing you with Kayla's crazy ass." She turned up her nose at the thought.

"Hell no, I don't want her either."

"You can play hard all you want to, but you love Alexus. Your ego is bruised and you're letting your pride get in the way of being with her."

"This has nothing to do with pride. I caught her in bed with another nigga. And I'm supposed to take her back after that?" I was getting upset that I was being looked at like the guilty one.

"She made a mistake TJ. People do it every day. I'm not saying that it's right, but it's done and it can't be undone."

"You like her, so I expect you to say that."

"Do you know why I like her? Because she reminds me a lot of myself," my mama said, asking, then answering her own question.

"I don't see how. You ain't no hoe. You and Lex are nothing alike." I started eating the food that she sat in front of me.

"Don't be so quick to speak until you know all of the facts."

"Whatever; if this baby is mine, then that's the only thing that we'll have to talk about. Other than that, I'm done with her. I refuse to take care of another man's child."

"You're upset right now, but you don't mean that. You are your father's child and you are just like him in every way."

"What do you mean by that?"

"I asked you to come over here because I wanted to talk to you about something important. It might, like it might not, change things between you and Alexus, but I just want to tell you my story." I was curious about what she was about to say so I sat up straight and gave her my undivided attention.

"Your daddy and I got married when you were only two years old. During that time, he was just starting to get his business off the ground, so he worked long hours and was hardly ever home. After doing that for so long, I started to get lonely and bored with being home by myself all the time. So, on weekends when you were staying with your grandparents, I went out with a friend of mine and I ended up meeting someone."

"Wait, so what are you saying?" I interrupted her in the middle of her conversation.

"Stop interrupting me and just listen. Like I said, I met someone. We started out just talking on the phone but, after a while, we started hanging out and spending time together. It didn't take long before things got physical and we ended up being intimate with one another."

"Man, I don't want to hear this," I said as I pushed the plate of food that I was eating to the side.

My appetite was gone after listening to all the shit that she was telling me. I stood up and prepared to exit stage left.

"Tyree, just sit down and hear me out," she pleaded.

"No, you're telling me that you cheated on my father and you want me to sit here and listen to this shit!" I was furious but the look on her face let me know that I'd gone too far.

"Watch your damn mouth! If you just listen, you'll understand what I'm trying to tell your stubborn ass!"

I was never one to be disrespectful towards my elders, so I sat back down and allowed her to continue.

"Ok, so why do I need to know that you cheated?"

"I'm getting to that if you just shut up. So, anyway, after a few months of going back and forth, your father ended up finding out about us. We separated for a little while, but I also ended the affair that I was having. After being apart for about a month, your father and I decided to work things out and get back together. Not long after that, I found out that I was pregnant with your sisters. And just like Alexus, I didn't know who I was pregnant for at the time. When the twins were born, we took a paternity test and found out that they were not for your father."

I swear, I felt like the air had been sucked right out of me. I know that she wasn't sitting here telling me that my sisters and I didn't have the same father. That had to be a lie. He had them spoiled rotten. Hell, he damn near treated them better than he treated me sometimes. I had a million questions, but I didn't know where to start.

"So, who is their father?" That was the first question that came to mind.

"His name was Ivan and he was an army vet."

"What do you mean was? Where is he now?"

"He died in a car accident when the twins were only six months old. Your daddy adopted them a few months later and we've been one big happy family ever since."

"Do they know?" I asked, referring to the twins.

"No, and the only reason why I told you is because I see that you're going through the exact same thing. You would have never known had I not told you, and you never looked at me as a bad person. I just need you to understand that good people sometimes make bad decisions."

"I get what you're saying, but this is different. You don't have to worry about the twins' daddy coming around trying to be in their lives. If this baby is for Alexus' ex, he'll be around twenty-four seven. It's not about the baby with him; he's in love with Alexus. I just can't deal with that."

"I would just hate for you to give up without even trying." I couldn't lie; she really gave me a lot to think about. I really did love Alexus, but I didn't know if I would ever be able to trust her again.

"Honestly, I feel stupid for even feeling like I still want to be with her after what she did."

"Pride is the sign of a foolish man," my mama said as she grabbed my hand and pulled me outside.

I saw Alexus sitting in a lounge chair, reading a book on her iPad. I walked over to her and sat on the edge of the chair. I knew that she saw me, but she never looked up or acknowledged my presence. I grabbed her feet and started giving her a massage.

"Stop!" she yelled before taking her feet out of my lap.

"Sorry about not speaking to you last night."

I grabbed her feet once again. This time, she didn't move them away.

"It's cool; I didn't want you to get in trouble with your girlfriend," she replied in her usual sassy tone that I missed so much.

"That's not my girlfriend but let me find out that you're jealous." She returned my smile but didn't reply to what I said. I guess I got my answer and she was indeed jealous. She was so pretty and I felt like I could stare at her forever.

"I find out what I'm having when I go back to the doctor next week," she said, breaking me away from the trance that she had me in.

"I know, I'll be there."

I really wanted to take my mama's advice and move forward, but it wasn't that easy for me. Alexus had hurt me in a way that no other woman ever had. I would just hate for us to have a repeat of what happened before. I looked up and saw my sisters and Jada looking at us, smiling. I knew that us being together was what Alexus and everybody else wanted, but I just had to be sure that it was what I wanted too.

Chapter 13

I'd been at the club for over four hours and had yet to make one hundred dollars. One of the regulars was having a party and he requested who he wanted to dance for him. Of course, I wasn't chosen, but that didn't bother me too much. I was pissed because some of the other patrons who weren't a part of the party decided to join in with them as well, cutting the few tips we did get short.

It was only about four of us who weren't invited to dance and we were being completely ignored. After a while of getting no action, I got fed up and decided to call it a night. When the club was popping, sometimes I wouldn't get home until after three in the morning. Right now, it was only a little after eleven and I was about to leave.

I went to the locker room and started changing into my

regular clothes when Lisa came in and started talking to me. Lisa and I used to work at the nursing home together and she was the one who got me on at the strip club. Her brother was a bouncer, so she knew just about everyone who came in. She wasn't the prettiest girl I knew, but she had a shape that I would die for so, of course, she was chosen to dance at the private party.

"Are you leaving already?" she asked when she saw me getting dressed.

"Hell yeah, I'm not making any money, so there's no need for me to stay."

"Where's Ayanna?"

"She's spending the day with her kids."

At least that was what she told me. I wanted to tell her that I didn't know or care where she was, but I held my tongue.

Lisa and Ayanna were close, so I didn't need her going back and telling her that I was talking about her. And Lisa was messy enough to do just that. I didn't know why, but Ayanna had been acting kind of funny for the past few weeks. She never wanted to do any private shows with me and we barely spoke when we did see each other. She was still living with Troy and I, but she was hardly there unless it was to shower or sleep.

"Oh, ok. I knew it was a reason why she wasn't out there making that money."

"There's not much money to be made. That's why I'm going home."

"Girl, you must be crazy. I've made over six hundred dollars so far."

"Well, I haven't even made one hundred," I replied honestly.

"You're a cute girl, Keanna, but you need to invest in you some butt injections or something. I told Ayanna the same thing. Y'all work in a strip club. The nicer your body is, the more money you make. Nobody is going to pay top dollar to watch y'all shaking them flat asses," she said, laughing.

That must have been what she was doing because her ass was almost detached from her body.

"Whatever, I don't have a problem any other time," I replied defensively.

"Alright, don't get mad at me for telling the truth." She raised her hands in mock surrender. I didn't feel like going back and forth with her, so I didn't respond. Instead, I grabbed my duffel bag and headed for the back entrance. Since being caught off guard by Alexus, I made sure that I had my stun gun ready and waiting whenever I walked through the parking lot. I had to wear heavy makeup for two weeks to cover the black eye and bruises that I was left with after that fight. I walked to my car, looking in all directions until I was safely inside.

I was so aggravated with the amount of money that I made today. I just wanted to take a shower and get in my bed. Hopefully, the next day would be much better. I pulled up to our apartments and sat out front for a while. Sometimes, I hated going inside because I never knew how Troy was going to act. He had a million personalities and I never knew which one was going to show up at any given time.

And, lately, it'd only been getting worse. He started staying out later than usual and, some nights, he wouldn't even come home at all. When he was there, he hardly slept in the bed with me. He was always on the sofa or in the recliner. We had no sex life at all. The most action I'd seen over the past few weeks was when Ayanna and I did our private shows. Since she'd been on her bullshit lately, even that had stopped.

Even Malik was acting like he was too busy these days. When I was breaking him off, he made sure that he had time for me. Now, I almost had to make an appointment to see him.

After a while of feeling sorry for myself, I grabbed my bag and headed inside. It was almost midnight, so I knew that Troy wasn't home, if he planned to come home at all. As soon as I opened the door, my nostrils were assaulted by a sweet smell that I couldn't identify. I heard music playing in the dining room, so I made my way down the hall. I didn't know what to expect, so I grabbed my Taser, just in case I needed it. My heart was almost beating out of my chest, the closer I got. There was a small flicker of light that came from the crack in the door. I heard voices, but I couldn't make out who they belonged to. When I approached the door, I peeked inside before I opened it.

That was a huge mistake. A huge lump formed in my throat as I saw Ayanna dressed in nothing but a thong and bra, dancing around the room to the music that was playing. Dressed in only his boxers, Troy sat in a chair smiling, while throwing crumpled up money at her feet. It felt like I was stuck in place. My entire body was frozen with a mixture of rage and hurt.

Ayanna was the first real female friend that I ever had, or so I thought. I kept looking as she stopped dancing momentarily and grabbed something from the almost empty book shelf. She walked back over to Troy and got down on her knees. In her hand was a mirror lined with white powder that they both wasted no time sucking up their nostrils. I was in total shock. Troy tried to get me to do drugs several times, but I never did. Drugs were something that I swore to never indulge in, especially since they were the reason that I no longer had a mother.

But, just like Cherika, Ayanna seemed to be a willing participant when it came to pleasing my man. I looked on as they made each line on the mirror disappear. I almost threw up when Troy pulled her up and stuck his tongue down her throat. That was it, I'd seen enough. I kicked the door open with my foot and made it slam hard into the wall behind it.

"What the fuck is going on in here!" I yelled as I flipped on the lights. As loaded as they were, it was hard for me to read the expressions on their faces. I didn't know if they were shocked or scared. Troy jumped up faster than he should have and went crashing to the floor. He was up just as fast as he went down and came rushing over to me. Ayanna grabbed a pillow from the sofa and tried to cover her half-naked body.

"What are you doing home so early baby?" Troy asked while rubbing his nose profusely.

"Are you fucking serious right now, Troy? After everything that I've done for you and this is how you repay me?" I said in between sobs.

"And bitch, I'm the reason why you're not living under the fucking bridge!" I charged at Ayanna but Troy pulled me back before I had a chance to get to her.

"Chill out Keanna, it's not even that serious." Troy laughed like something was really funny.

"You think this shit is a fucking game!" I yelled as I started swinging wildly on him. He grabbed my hands and held them above my head, preventing me from hitting him.

"Let me go!" I screamed to the top of my lungs. The tears were blinding me, but I still had my eyes on my targets.

"Calm down and I'll let you go," Troy said, trying to hold me down.

"I can't believe that y'all did this to me."

I was crying my heart out. I was heartbroken. No matter who came and went, I was always there for Troy, no matter what happened. I knew he'd cheated on me before, but I never had to witness it. After a few minutes, I'd calmed down enough for Troy to let me go. I was still pissed with him, but I turned my anger to my, now, ex friend.

"Get out! I don't give a damn if you don't have anywhere else to go. I want you the fuck out of this house now!" I yelled at Ayanna.

"Nah, she's not going anywhere," Troy said calmly. I must have been hearing things because I know he didn't just say what I thought he said.

"What?" I wanted him to repeat himself, just to be sure I was hearing the right thing.

"I said that she's not going anywhere." He repeated himself like it was no big deal.

"Are you serious right now? You're choosing her over me?" I was in disbelief.

"No, I'm not choosing anybody. I don't want you to go either."

"You must out of your damn mind if you think I'm staying here with her. I want her gone!"

"Like I just said, nobody's leaving," Troy said with finality.

"I am," I said, praying that he would stop me. He knew that I didn't have anywhere else to go.

"You were the one who wanted her to dance for me and now you're pissed because she did it."

"You know this is not what I wanted. We were supposed to dance for you together at the club, not one on one in our house. Stop being so fucking stupid!"

"You better watch your damn mouth." He stepped closer to me like he was about to swing.

"Look, it's either her or me. You can't have us both. I'm not sharing a man." I looked from Troy to Ayanna, waiting for him to choose.

After all of the years that I've put in with him, he better make the right choice, I thought.

"Fuck this, I'm leaving," Ayanna said, walking past us.

I was about to get happy until Troy reached out his hand and pulled her back. I was devastated. In a matter of months, another woman had managed to come in between something that it took me years to build. I was the same one who nursed him back to health a few weeks ago when Dre almost killed him with his bare hands. I was the same one who paid every bill in this house because his broke ass couldn't afford to. As much as it hurt, I refused to shed any more tears. I looked over at Ayanna's smiling face and I actually had murder on my mind. I knew that Troy wasn't worth it, but it was just the principal.

"You just remember that leaving was your choice," Troy said as he started putting on his clothes.

Just then, I remembered the Taser that I slipped into my pocket right before I busted up their little party. I pulled it out and aimed it right at Ayanna. Without even thinking about it, I pulled the trigger and watched as her body dropped to the floor and shook uncontrollably.

"What the fuck!" Troy yelled as he jumped up and came after me.

I didn't hesitate when I turned the Taser towards him and gave him a dose of electricity as well. His body fell to the floor as a puddle of his urine made its way to the carpet right along with him. I didn't look back when I grabbed my bag and ran for the door with only the clothes on my body.

It was almost two in the morning and I was driving around aimlessly with nowhere to go. I had a few dollars on me and a little more in the bank, but I didn't want to spend it on a room. I didn't know when I would be able to get my clothes, so I would probably have to use that money to buy some more. I was back on speaking terms with my family, but it was too late to call them or show up at their house unannounced.

Dre still wasn't fucking with me and I was too scared to call my uncle EJ. Until now, I never realized just how alone I was. I didn't have any real friends to call on in my time of need. Then, just that quick, Malik came to mind. I'd helped him out more times than I could count; now, it was his time to return the favor. I scrolled through my phone until I came up on the name 'Mary'. That was the name that I had Malik's number saved under so Troy wouldn't get suspicious. I dialed the number and waited for him to pick up.

"Hello," he answered in a groggy, but angry voice.

"Malik, I know it's late and I'm sorry for calling, but I really need your help," I said desperately.

"Are you out of your fucking mind calling me this time of the morning?" He sounded like he was wide awake now and fully alert. I could tell that he was angry but I needed his help.

"I'm sorry for calling so late, but I didn't know who else to call. I have a problem."

"So, what does that have to do with me?" I wanted to go off, but I really needed him so I decided keep quiet.

"I know it's a lot to ask, but do you think your sister would mind if I crashed on her sofa for a few hours. Troy and I had it out and I left. I just need to sleep for a few hours and I'll be gone; I promise."

"What! Girl, you must be crazy. I barely have somewhere to stay and you want me to ask if you can come here too!"

"Malik, please. I've never asked you for anything. Just do this one thing for me," I begged.

The phone went silent and I assumed he was giving my request some thought. After another minute of more silence, I looked at my phone, only to see that he'd already hung up on me. I was pissed but, most of all, I was tired of every man in my life walking all over me. All my life I'd been a giver, and every man I met had no problem taking whatever I had to offer. Troy had already been on the receiving end of my wrath; now, it was time for me to show Malik that I was not the weak bitch that he took me for.

I made a U-turn in the middle of the street and headed in the direction of his sister's house. I knew the street, but I didn't know the exact house that she lived in. Malik would never let me pick him up in front of the house.

As soon as I turned on the street, I tried to look for anything that was familiar to me. I did remember Malik saying that his sister drove a silver SUV, so that was really the only clue that I had. I drove down the block, carefully looking on both sides of the street until I spotted what I was looking for. There was a silver Expedition parked in the driveway of a house near the end of the block. As I got closer to the house, I had to do a double take. I specifically remembered Malik telling me that his car had been repossessed, but here it was, parked on the opposite side of the driveway. There was no mistaking the all-black Altima with the Virginia license plates that I knew without a doubt belonged to him. Now, I was livid. For the second time in just a few hours, I'd been played for a fool. Unfortunately for them, today was not a good day to piss me off.

With my Taser in hand, I got out of my car and made my way to the front door. I hated to bring my drama to Malik's sister's house, but it was his own fault. I decided to try calling him once again before I woke up the entire house but, of course, he didn't answer. I pulled on the storm door, only to discover that it was locked. I used my open palm to bang on the door, while ringing the doorbell at the same time. He was going to learn today.

It only took a minute before I heard someone fumbling with the locks on the door. As soon as it opened, I was greeted with a scowl on the face of a very petite pregnant woman, who I assumed was Malik's sister.

"Can I help you?" she asked with her hand resting on her hip.

"Sorry to knock on your door so late, but can you call your brother to the door please?" I asked politely.

"My brother? I don't have a brother." She looked at me like I was stupid and that's exactly how I felt.

"Aren't you Malik's sister?" I was already dreading her answer.

"No sweetie, I'm Malik's fiancée. And who the hell are you?" She looked at me like she was dreading my answer as well.

It was official; this was just not my day. I saw Malik coming from the back of the house with fire in his eyes. He gently moved the pregnant woman to the side while he took her place at the door. He was saying something to her, but I couldn't make out exactly what he was saying. I cringed when

115

I saw how loving and sweet he was with her, compared to how he always tried to manhandle me. He gave her a soft peck on the lips before turning around to face me.

"Get the fuck away from my house before I have you arrested!" he yelled when he stepped onto the porch.

"I thought your car was repossessed and you were living with your sister. Nigga, you lied about everything that you told me! If you didn't want to be with me, you could have just told me instead of lying." I was furious and I had every right to be.

"Man, I never wanted to be with you and I never told you that I did. I have a family. I'm getting married in a year and my girl is about to have our first child in two months. You make it too easy for a nigga to lie to you!"

He yelled angrily, making me feel lower than I already felt. I didn't know why these things always seemed to happen to me. I was a good woman who deserved a good man. The problem was, I could never find one.

"Wow," was all I managed to get out after he revealed to me how he really felt. "So, I guess you were using me all this time, huh?"

"I never asked you for nothing. You were the one always offering to do things for me."

"Yeah, but you never turned it down either."

"Look, do us both a favor and leave. Make this your first and last time coming around here."

"Or what?" I asked defiantly. I was hurt and embarrassed. There was nothing more that he or anyone else could have done to me at this point. His girlfriend, or should I say his fiancée, came to the porch to see what was going on. I guess he decided to show out when he saw that she was watching.

"Just get the fuck off of my property and don't come back!" he yelled as he turned to walk away. Just like I did earlier, I reached into my front pocket and pulled out my Taser.

116

"Oh, my God!" Malik's fiancée yelled as the electricity from my Taser sent him flying to the ground.

I turned away and ran to my car when I saw her coming down from the porch. I jumped into my car and sped away as fast as I could. I drove about five blocks before I had to pull the car over to regain my composure. My body shook uncontrollably as I cried what felt like gallons of tears. Just a few months ago, it seemed as if things were looking up for me. Now, I felt like death was better than the pain that I was experiencing right now. I guess all the wrong I'd done in the past was finally catching up to me and I had to admit that it didn't feel good.

Chapter 14

To say my day started out bad was an understatement. I'd been calling Cherika all morning, but she had yet to answer. I'd been standing outside her door for twenty minutes, trying to convince her to let me get my kids for a few days. She was pissed because I hadn't called or been around for the past week to see them. I told her that I had a lot on my mind and I needed time to myself.

That was partially the truth. I did spend a few days at home by myself but, for the last two days, I'd been chilling in a hotel room with Mya. The one time we left out of the room to go get something to drink, we ran into her messy ass sister, Charde. Crazy thing was the hotel that we were staying in was over an hour away from home. That bitch, Charde, was like a walking talking GPS. Her ass really did get around.

"I don't have shit to say to you unless it's in front of a judge!" Cherika yelled through the locked front door. She'd been on her bullshit lately and I was really not in the mood for it.

"Girl, open this damn door before I kick this bitch down!" I yelled back.

"No. I'm tired of your lying ass."

I didn't want to scare my kids, but I was about two minutes away from making good on my promise.

"Cherika, can you stop being so childish and open the door."

"Hell no, you can't sweet talk your way out of this."

"Well, just let me see them. I don't have to take them if you don't want me to," I said, giving in to her temper tantrum.

"You must really think I'm stupid Dre."

"Man, I swear I'm not trying to do nothing stupid. I'm just tired of arguing with you."

I guess she had to think about it because it still took a few minutes before she finally opened the door. She stepped to the side and allowed me to come in.

"I shouldn't even let you see them. Obviously, they're not that important to you since one of your hoes always comes first."

Since I knew that replying would only make matters worse, I chose to ignore her ignorant ass.

"Where are they?" I asked, referring to my kids. She went to the bottom of the staircase and yelled for them to come down. Both of my daughters came running as soon as they were called, but my boys never showed up.

"Lil Dre and Drew are sleeping," Denim said before I had a chance to ask.

120

I sat around for about an hour, spending time with my girls. I waited until they went back upstairs before I decided to talk to Cherika.

"What's your problem now?" I wanted to know.

"You are my problem." She had her hand on her hip so I knew she was about to go off.

"How am I your problem? What did I do this time?"

"I'm tired of all the lying and cheating. You say you want us to work things out, but you're still running around with other females. It's bad enough that I have to deal with you having a baby on the way, but how much more do you expect me to take!"

"I keep telling you that this shit is not gonna happen overnight. You want instant results and that's not realistic."

"It's never gonna happen at all as long as you don't know how to keep your dick in your pants."

"I'm not doing anything wrong. Mya is just my friend."

"That's bullshit and you know it. I can't keep doing this Dre. I almost lost my mind behind you dealing with Alexus and I can't go through that again. Sometimes, I feel like the only reason you want to work things out with me is because she doesn't want you anymore."

I didn't respond because it was sad to say that she was right. True to her word, when Alexus said she was done with me, she really meant it. Unlike my wife, she had no problem permanently cutting me off.

"Look, I know that things are not gonna happen overnight, but you could at least try. I mean, I'm your wife and I don't even know where you live," Cherika said as she wiped away the tears that started falling.

It was always the same thing with her. She was dying to know where I lived, but that would never happen. Alexus was the only woman who knew where I rested my head and she would be the only one if I had anything to say about it. Even

Mya was on my back about bringing her to my house. I wasn't feeling her enough to even let her meet my family, so going to my house was out of the question.

"I am trying. Nothing I seem to do is good enough for you. You're not happy unless I'm with you twenty-four seven." I was getting aggravated with the entire discussion.

"That's because I can't trust you to do the right thing!"

I was so over this conversation. I still didn't understand how a person could fight so hard to be with someone that they didn't trust.

"I'm about to go," I announced. "When can I come and get my kids?"

"If you were really trying, you would come here to spend time with all of us instead of just taking them to your house," she said while looking at me.

She caught me off guard with that one. I know I told her a million times that I wanted us to try and work things out, but the truth was I just wasn't ready. If she would just give me so more time to figure some things out, everything would be all good. There was no point in voicing that to Cherika though. She didn't want to hear nothing that I had to say unless it included me saying that I was coming back home. That was the reason why I was always telling her what she wanted to hear. I hated lying to her, but she really gave me no other choice.

"We'll talk about it when I call you later," I said as I stood up to leave. As much as I didn't want to lie to her, I knew that she couldn't handle the truth.

As soon as I hopped in my truck, I called Alexus to see what was going on with her. She promised to call or text me at least once a week to let me know what was going on with her and the baby, but she hadn't been living up to her end of the bargain. If I didn't call her, I probably would never hear from her. It'd been over a week since she found out about the sex of the baby, and she had yet to call and tell me anything. Then, to make matters worse, she wasn't answering when I called her. Even now, I was being sent straight to voicemail. She must have thought I was playing when I said I would show up to wherever she was if I couldn't get in contact with her. I was about twenty minutes away, but I was on my way to her mother's house right now.

After stopping to get gas around the corner, I pulled up to Alexus' mother's house at the same time as another car. I took a minute to admire the newly-modeled silver Jaguar with custom rims and mirrored tints, until I saw who stepped out of it. I got pissed when I saw Alexus' boyfriend jump out of the driver's side and walk over to open the door for his passenger. When I saw him helping Alexus get out of the car, my anger was only intensified. Wasting no time, I got out of my truck and made my way over to them. I looked around and saw a few people outside, but I didn't give a damn. I was about to show my ass for the world to see.

"What, is your phone broke or something?" I asked as I walked up on Alexus and her boo. She looked up and saw me and her expression was priceless. Her face showed a mixture of anger and embarrassment as she looked into my eyes.

"No, my phone is not broke. I was going to text you later," she replied with her usual attitude.

"Yeah, right; you haven't sent one text since you told me that you would." I matched her mood with an attitude of my own.

"Well, I'll text you later." She tried to brush me off but I wasn't having it.

"Fuck that. I'm here, so you can talk to me now." I was getting rowdy but she left me no other choice.

"Let's go Lex," her lame ass boyfriend said as he grabbed her hand.

I was waiting for his ass to say something, so I could unleash my fury on him. After all, my anger wasn't aimed at Alexus; it was all for him. I didn't know what she saw in his pretty ass anyway.

"Nigga, mind your business. This don't have shit to do with you," I said as I stood in their way.

"Nigga, fuck you; she is my business." That was the last thing he said right before my fist connected with his jaw.

That was something that I'd wanted to do since I first found out that he was in the picture. He let Alexus' hand go and we went into an all-out boxing match.

"Dre, stop; are you crazy! Stop it!" Alexus screamed as she tried desperately to end what I had started.

I ignored her as I kept pounding my fist into her boyfriend's face. He was holding his own, but he couldn't match the powerful blows that I was throwing his way. I thought he would have fallen by now, but he surprised me by keeping his balance throughout the fight.

By now, Alexus was screaming for some of her neighbors to come and break us up. I didn't think anyone was listening but, after a minute, two men walked over and were able to pull us apart. I watched in disgust as she rushed to his aid, trying to make sure he was alright. I laughed inside as I watched him spit a wad of blood from his mouth onto the pavement. Besides the ringing in my ears and my torn shirt, I didn't look too bad when I inspected myself through the mirror of my truck.

"Get the fuck off of me!" I heard Alexus' boyfriend yelling at her.

"What? Why are you mad with me?" she asked him in shock. He grabbed his keys that had fallen to the ground and headed towards his car.

"Everything that's happening is your fault. I'm a grown ass man and you got me out here fighting like a damn child. I don't have time for this shit!" He hopped into his car and sped off.

"Tyree, wait!" Alexus yelled. I wanted to go slap some sense into her stupid ass for standing there begging that nigga to come back. Even though I knew she was pissed, I walked over to her anyway.

"I'm sorry," I said when I was standing in front of her. I felt like shit when I saw the tears pouring from her eyes. I reached out to touch her and she completely went off on me.

"Don't touch me! You're always saying that you're sorry but, sometimes, sorry isn't enough. You were sorry when you use to hit me. Sorry when you cheated on your wife. Sorry when you got caught in a lie. You're always sorry about something!"

I didn't reply because she was too upset to listen to anything that I had to say.

"I'm begging you to, please, just leave me alone," she said, breaking my heart.

"All I asked you to do was call or text to let me know what was going on with you and the baby, and you couldn't even do that. You're trying to shut me out, but you let this nigga come to all of your appointments and everything else. And that probably ain't even his baby anyway."

"I pray to God that it's not yours."

She was trying her best to get to me, and I was trying my best not to let her. I was failing miserably because her words really did hurt.

"When the baby gets here, I'll let you know so we can do the test. Other than that, please stay away from me." She tried to walk off but she had me fucked up. I pulled her ass right back and made her listen to what I had to say.

"No, fuck that! You're keeping him informed and got him going to appointments and shit. You not gon' play me like that. I have just as much right as he does when it comes to this baby. Until it's proven that it's not mine, I want to know everything that's going on."

"Keep your hands off of me," she said as she pulled away from me. I hadn't noticed before, but her stomach was way bigger than it was the last time I saw her. She had that glow that all pregnant women had and it made her even prettier than she already was.

"So, what are you having? You were supposed to call and tell me when you found out."

"It's a boy." She looked away when she replied.

"Look, I apologize for not keeping you informed and I'll try to do better with that. I'll even make sure I answer when you call, but you can't just show up here whenever you feel like it."

"Well, if you keep your end of the bargain, I won't have to."

"I just told you that I would. I'm going inside. I've had enough drama for one day," she said, walking off.

I watched her until she made it inside before getting in my truck and pulling off. I didn't show my emotions in front of her, but I was excited to know that I would possibly be having another son. I just hoped like hell that he was mine. I knew without a doubt that, if this baby wasn't mine, Alexus was gone for good. I hated to admit that the same kind of hold she had on me was the same kind of hold that Tyree had on her.

Chapter 15

For the past two weeks, things seemed to be looking up for me. School was going good, and Dre and I seemed to be in a good place. We still weren't where I wanted us to be, but at least we were making some progress. And, now, I was really excited because he finally agreed to come to the house and spend a few nights with me and our kids. He still didn't want to go back to counseling, but I was hopeful that I would get him to change his mind about that one day too. He was really trying and I had to give him credit for that.

On the other hand, my mama was not too pleased when she found out that my husband and I were trying to reconcile. Thanks to my big mouth sisters, she knew everything that was going on. They told her about Alexus' pregnancy and about us running into her at church. She was also convinced that Dre only wanted to be with me because Alexus didn't want him anymore, but I didn't believe that to be true. I was sure by the time they finished filling her head up, she probably hated Dre even more now than she did before. She kept telling me that the devil came in all forms and Dre was a devil in disguise. I stopped going to church with her again and she said that he was to blame for me falling back into my old ways.

Of course, I wasn't trying to hear it. If anything, getting my family back was going to keep me happy and not depressed like I'd been for the past few months. I'd even accepted the fact that he might have another mouth to feed once Alexus' baby came. I didn't like it, but I couldn't change what was already done.

Even though she was driving me crazy with her dislike for my husband, I still agreed to go with my mother and sisters to bring my kids on an outing today.

My kids had been dying to go play laser tag, so they were excited to finally be going today. It was rare for my mother to get any time off. Between her job as a nurse and her dedication to the church, most of her time was always accounted for. I was surprised to find out that she took two weeks off from work and didn't have anything planned. She said the only thing she wanted to do was spend some time with her kids and grandkids.

I pulled up to my mother's house, and my kids jumped out of the car before I had a chance to put it in park. My mom had an SUV, so we were all going to be riding with her. Before getting out of the car, I said a silent prayer that things would go smoothly today. My sisters and I did things together all the time, but it'd been a while since our mother joined us. We all loved her dearly but, sometimes, she was just too critical. I think she was even harder on me because I was the only one out of the three of us who had kids. I was also the only one of her kids who had ever been married. My sisters, especially Charde, got around a lot, so I didn't think marriage was ever in their future. I, on the other hand, wanted nothing more than to be a wife and have a family.

"Hey everybody," I said when I walked through the front door. My sisters were sitting in the living room watching tv. I didn't see my mama or my kids, so I figured they were upstairs.

"Hey girl, you're looking cute today," Cherice said. I playfully twirled around to show her my entire outfit before I sat down on the sofa in between them. Charde was on the phone, so she didn't pay much attention to us.

"Where's mama?" I asked.

"She was still getting dressed. I'm sure your kids are up there rushing her."

Just as the words left her mouth, we heard all of them trampling down the staircase.

"We're ready!" Denim announced in her usual loud voice.

"Hey mama, I know they probably dragged you out of your room."

I laughed when I saw that her shoes weren't tied and her shirt was buttoned up wrong.

"They sure did. One of y'all will have to drive while I get myself together. I haven't even combed my hair yet," she complained. I offered to drive her truck as we all got up and headed out of the front door.

As soon as we pulled up to the building that housed the laser tag, my children were ready to jump out of the truck.

"Wait a minute! When y'all get in there, I want everybody to stay together. Y'all make sure to hold Drew's hand wherever y'all go." I had to give them some instructions before we went inside. The place only had one way in and one way out, so I wasn't worried about them going anywhere. I was going to be sitting right near the door. When we walked inside, the place was kind of crowded, but there were still a lot of tables available.

"Y'all find a table while I go and pay for them to play some games," my mama told us.

"Ok, let's find a table close to the door, so I can make sure my brats don't try to leave up out of here," I replied.

It didn't take long for us to find two tables close enough for us to push together. We sat down and got comfortable, while my mama ordered the food and made sure that the kids were straight.

"So, what's going on with you and that husband of yours?" Cherice asked.

"Not much is going on. We're trying to get things back on track, but we're taking our time."

"Taking your time with what?" my mother asked when she came back to the table.

"She's talking about Dre's dog ass," Charde answered sarcastically.

"Watch your mouth," my mother scolded while pointing at my sister. "But, what about Dre?"

"Nothing. Cherice just asked what was going on with us." I no longer wanted to discuss it and I was praying that she just let it go.

"Hopefully, nothing, but this is not the time or place to discuss all of that," she said, waving us off. I breathed a sigh of relief when she changed the subject and started talking about something else.

A little over an hour later, we had all eaten and were just sitting at the table talking. I had to round up my kids to make them sit down for a while and eat the pizza that was ordered for them. As soon as they were done, they ran off to play some more games. They were almost out of game tokens, so I knew it would only be a matter of time before they came back to beg for more.

And just like I thought, I saw my oldest daughter heading in our direction with her sister and brothers following close behind.

"I guess I need to buy some more tokens," my mama said, laughing.

We were all laughing with her until my children got closer to us. The smile on my face faded when I saw that each one of my kids had a huge bucket overflowing with tokens that I knew none of us had purchased.

"Where did y'all get those tokens from?" my mother asked in a panic.

"My daddy's friend bought them for us," Lil Dre said happily.

My heart dropped as I looked around to see just who they were referring to. I knew they weren't talking about any of his male friends because they would have made their presence known if they were here. The first person that came to mind was Alexus, but they knew her. They would have called her by name if she was who they were referring to. I hated Dre for always involving my kids with him and his other women. It was bad enough that he was doing wrong in the first place.

"That's her right there," Denim said, pointing the woman out. When I looked in the direction that she pointed, I almost died when I spotted Mya standing there smiling at me. As if I wasn't already pissed off, the bitch had the nerve to wave at me.

"That's the girl that I told you I saw Dre with," Charde said louder than she needed to.

"Give me those tokens," I said, taking all of them away from my kids. I jumped up and headed over to where she was standing and, of course, my sisters followed me. I had only seen Mya once when I went to visit Dre at the facility that he was in, but I remembered her face just like it was yesterday.

"Y'all come back here. This is not the time or place for this foolishness and especially not in front of these kids!" my mother yelled. We ignored her and kept moving towards our target.

"Here you go," I said, shoving the buckets of tokens in her hand. "I don't need or want you to do a damn thing for my kids. As a matter of fact, do me a favor and stay the fuck away from them."

"What's up wifey?" Mya asked with a smile. She was standing there with another woman who immediately started laughing when she made the comment.

"No, bitch, you got the wrong one. I'm the wife."

"My fault, you are the wife; I'm wifey." She laughed and I was ready to knock her the fuck out.

Before I had a chance to reply or react, Charde reached over me and grabbed Mya by her hair. I saw my mother running towards us, but it was already too late. Mya's friend jumped in and helped her, which made Cherice and I jump in to help our sister. I really wasn't worried about Mya's friend because I had my sights set on her. I heard my kids screaming and the other patrons were doing their best to get out of the way as we fought like wild animals in the middle of the floor.

"Stop this, y'all need to be ashamed of yourselves!"

My mother was screaming as she tried to pull us apart. When Mya's friend fell, Charde took it upon herself to finish her off, while Cherice and I beat Mya out of the shirt and bra that she was wearing. Some of the male workers immediately rushed over and did their best to pull us apart. When the staff was finally able to separate us, they had to give Mya a souvenir t-shirt to cover the naked top half of her body.

"You guys have to leave. The police have already been called," the manager said when he walked over to us.

"Let's get out of here before I have to bail all of you out of jail," my mother frowned in disgust.

"Bitch, I'm not Alexus! I'm not going nowhere; you can trust and believe that. My daddy was a married man, so I don't mind sharing!" Mya was screaming to the top of her lungs, sounding stupid.

I didn't even waste my time replying. I gathered up my kids and their belongings and made my way to the exit.

"Is this what you plan to be doing for the rest of your life? Fighting over a man that you're supposed to be married to," my mama said as she stood in front of me.

"Not now, ma. I swear, I am not in the mood for all of this." I fought back tears as I made my way to the exit.

"I don't care what you're in the mood for. This is ridiculous. You can't even have a relaxing day with your family without running into one of your husband's mistresses. And it's not right for y'all to involve these kids in all that mess."

"I wasn't the one who started it. Charde hit her first."

Sometimes, I had to wonder if Charde was really fighting for me or did she have her own motives. There were times when she would be more upset about Dre's affairs than I was.

"You're missing the whole point Cherika. What I'm saying is it wouldn't have happened in the first place if your so-called husband was doing right by you. I promise you; you're going to regret the day that you ever married D'Andre Mack and you can mark my words," my mother said with finality.

I never thought I'd see the day that I agreed with anything that my mother had to say about my husband but, today, I did. I was actually starting to regret the day that ever married D'Andre Mack.

Chapter 16

It'd been about two weeks since Alexus' ex, Dre, and I had a fight. I started out blaming her for everything, but I knew that it really wasn't her fault. I'd be the first to admit that she'd been trying her best to be honest with me about everything. She told me about every time he called or sent her a text. As much as I couldn't stand his conniving ass, I understood him wanting to know about the baby because I felt the exact same way.

Alexus wasn't buying it though. She felt like he was just trying to get close to her and using the baby as an excuse. Knowing his stalking ass, that was probably true. I could tell that he was used to having things go his way because he couldn't seem to take no for an answer. He just popped up whenever he felt like doing so and it was driving Alexus crazy.

I was trying my best not to stress her out, but he was doing the exact opposite.

Alexus was five months pregnant now and I didn't want to miss anything. I was there for every appointment ever since it was confirmed that she was pregnant. Even though we hadn't officially agreed that we were back together, it felt like we were. She was even starting to spend some nights at my house again and I hated it when she had to leave. The only thing that drove me crazy was her getting up at all times of the night to run to the bathroom. I really felt bad for her because she never got to sleep long before she had to go again.

In just the short time that we were apart, I'd seen the changes in her and I like what I'm seeing so far. She seemed to have matured since she found out that she was pregnant. I was proud of the woman that she was becoming.

With her clinicals and graduation a little over two months away, she had a lot on her plate. Not to mention, she would be having the baby not long after that. My mama and my sisters were already planning her baby shower to be held two weeks after she graduated. By then, she would be eight months pregnant. I told them that I would foot the bill for anything they needed because I really wanted everything to be nice.

Since it was a nice day outside, I decided to ride my bike instead of taking one of my cars. I didn't get to ride it that often, so I jumped at the chance to do so. I wanted to hit up the mall early before Alexus and I went to the movies later. As soon as I backed the bike out of my garage, my phone started ringing to the tone that was set for my pops. As soon as I answered, I regretted my decision to do so. He always had a way of changing my plans.

"What's up pops?" I asked when I answered the phone.

"Hey, I need you to do me a big favor. I'm tied up in a meeting and I know I won't make it on time," he said in a hurry.

"Alright, what's up?"

"I need you to go to my house and get the papers for the building that Sheila just purchased from us. I've already made the copies and left them in my office. Just give her the folder with her name on it and everything is already in there."

I was quiet on the other end because I really wanted to tell him no. Sheila was Kayla's mother and I really didn't want to see her or her daughter. I hadn't seen Kayla since I spent the night at the hotel with her all those weeks ago. She called me a few times, but she never got an answer. I really wanted to make things work with Alexus and there was no room for anyone else.

"Did you hear what I said boy?" my pops asked after I didn't reply.

"Yeah, I heard you. I'm on my way over there now," I replied, sounding unsure.

I was going to get her folder and wait for her ass on the front porch. No need for the pleasantries; I wanted her to get her shit and be gone. My mama was spending the day with my grandmother and I didn't know where the hell my sisters were. This was one time I wished somebody was home, so I didn't have to deal with the foolishness.

I hated talking to Kayla's mama just as much as I hated talking to her. She was always telling me that I was the perfect man for her daughter and I always had to stop myself from laughing. Kayla was cool when it came to sex, but that was as far as it would ever go with us. The first day I met her, she gave me oral sex and I'd been turned off from anything but sex from her ever since.

I got excited when I pulled up to my parents' house and saw my mama's car parked out front. But, then, I remembered that my aunt picked her up and I got pissed off all over again. I rolled my bike to the back of the house and entered through the back door. As soon as I got inside, I headed straight to my father's office in search of Ms. Sheila's folder. Finding it wasn't as easy as he made it seem, so I had to call him to ask him for more directions.

Of course, he didn't answer; that would have been too perfect if he did. I opened his file cabinet at the same time that the doorbell rang. That cancelled out my original plan to keep her outside. It would have been rude of me not to let her in, no matter how much I didn't want to.

I did a slow jog from my father's office in the back to go answer the door. Without asking who it was, I opened the door to find Kayla standing there. I was tempted to slam it right in her face, but the gentleman in me wouldn't let me do it.

"Where's your mama?" I asked, looking behind her.

"She wasn't feeling good, so she asked me to come over for her."

"Well, stay right here. I'll be right back with your papers." I attempted to walk away but she stopped me before I could.

"It's hot out here. Can I at least sit in the living room?"

I guess she was hot, wearing all that black in the middle of summer.

"Yeah, come in," I said against my better judgment.

I grabbed the remote and turned on the tv for her before I left out of the room. I went to search for the folder again but still came up empty. I was calling my pops one more time and, if he didn't answer, that was all on his ass. I was gonna kick Kayla's ass out and head to the mall like I planned to do. I had the phone on speaker while I looked through some more folders that were scattered on his desk. When the answering machine came on again, I hung up the phone and prepared to leave.

"Do you need some help?" Kayla asked, appearing in the doorway.

I didn't hear her approaching because the surround sound radio system that my pops installed in his office was on. Actually, he never turned it off. He said the old-school music that he listened to helped him relax when he was in here.

"No, I don't need any help. And who the hell told you to come back here? You better be lucky that my sisters aren't here."

"I'm not scared of your sisters and I don't know why you think I am."

"Whatever; but tell your mama that I can't find her paperwork, so she'll have to get with my pops to get another copy of everything."

"I told you that I can help you look." She walked over to me and I took a step back.

"I don't need any help. The shit is not in here," I replied, getting aggravated.

"Why don't you ever answer the phone when I call you?"

"Man, I don't wanna talk about that right now. It's time for you to go."

"Just give me five minutes of your time," she begged as she closed the door and walked closer to me. I was about to go off until she started massaging the bulge that sat in between my legs.

"Five minutes and I promise, I'll leave." She licked her thick, overly glossed lips and had my dick jumping.

She didn't even give me a chance to respond before she dropped to her knees and started undoing my pants. Once she got them down to my ankles, she started massaging my erection with both of her tiny hands, while she looked directly into my eyes.

"Don't pull out, I'm swallowing everything," she said just before she took my entire length to the back of her throat.

Chapter 17

I was only five months pregnant, but I was lazy as hell. I had a lot going on in the next few months, so I had to actually push myself to get everything done. I was so grateful to Tyree for everything that he was doing to help me. He made sure that I was doing everything that I needed to do in order to graduate in the next couple of months. We weren't all the way official yet, but we were working hard at getting there.

It didn't help that Dre was doing everything in his power to ruin it for me. After he and Tyree fought, it took me a while to get Tyree to forgive me, even though I didn't do anything wrong. We had finally gotten back on track and I wanted it to stay that way. I loved the way things were with us right now. Sometimes, we would stay up all night just to talk. I told him the entire story of how I ended up messing with Dre again. I also told him how I felt about his friendship with Mikayla.

It felt good with us being open and honest with each other. I knew that I hurt him by cheating on him with Dre. That was the reason why I didn't press him about us being in a relationship again. Even though I wanted that more than anything, I had to give him time. I already trusted him, but I wanted him to be able to trust me the same.

There were no more secrets with me. I told him everything, even if he didn't ask. There was no doubt in my mind that he was who I wanted to be with. The only thing that scared me was the paternity of my baby. I didn't want anything to do with Dre, so I was praying that he wasn't the father. He was already saying *his* baby, like he knew for sure it was his. Tyree told me that he didn't care who the father was, he was going to be there for me regardless, and that only made me love him more.

"Come on fat girl," Jada said as he helped me up from my chair.

I really didn't need any help, but she did things like that to be funny. My stomach was huge for me to be only five months, but I had no trouble getting around. My appetite was off the chain and I never felt like I was full. Like, right now, Jada, the twins, and I were leaving from a restaurant. Tyree was taking me to dinner and a movie later, but I couldn't wait that long to eat.

"Girl move, I can get up by myself," I said as I swatted her hand away.

"Are you sure that's only one baby in there?" She rubbed my stomach like she had doubts.

"Hell yeah, one healthy baby boy."

"Damn!" Trina yelled while looking in her purse.

"What?" all of us asked at the same time.

"I left my phone at home. I'm not going another step until I get it."

"Girl, all of us have a phone. Just use one of ours," Tina said.

"No, I want my own phone. I probably missed a million calls by now."

"I don't care where we go, as long as I don't have to drive," I noted.

We were in my car, but everybody else was taking turns driving. When we went to the nail shop earlier, it was Jada behind the wheel.

"I'll drive," Trina offered as she picked up my keys.

We all piled into my car in route to the twins' house. And just like always, my bladder was overflowing.

"I have to pee," I announced as we pulled up in the driveway.

"Damn, you just went to the bathroom right before we left the restaurant," Jada said.

"I know but this damn baby must be sleeping on my bladder." I got out of the car and wobbled towards the house.

"We might as well get out too," Jada said as she and Tina joined us at the front door.

When Trina opened the door, I ran straight for the bathroom in the hallway. I didn't think I would be able to make it to the one upstairs.

"Who left the damn tv on?" Trina asked to no one in particular.

She grabbed the remote and turned it off before she went upstairs in search of her phone. After emptying my bladder, I joined Tina and Jada in the kitchen. When Trina came back down with her phone, we were all ready to go.

"Let me grab a bottle of water," Jada said right before we left.

"Get me one too," I said, walking over to her.

"Your ass don't need nothing to drink as much as you pee," Tina said, laughing.

"They don't even have any water in here," Jada said, closing the refrigerator.

"My daddy might have some in his office. Come on, we can leave out of the back door," Trina said, walking in that direction.

We all followed her to her father's office to grab some water before we left. When she opened the door, I felt like I was about to faint when I saw Kayla on her knees with Tyree's dick shoved in her mouth.

"You nasty bitch!" Trina yelled before she ran in the office and went straight for Kayla. Jada and Tina were not too far behind, as they tried to stop her before she got too close.

"Oh shit!" Tyree said while trying to fix his clothes. The entire room started spinning and I actually felt like I was suffocating.

"Let me go!" Kayla yelled as Trina pulled her hair and dragged her out of the room. She was swinging wildly, as Trina pounded her fist hard into her face. It took Jada and Tina a minute, but they were finally able to pull Trina off her.

"Get your nasty ass out of our house!" Trina yelled, out of breath.

Kayla grabbed her purse from the floor, stumbling over her own feet as she hurriedly made her way through the house and out the front door.

"Tyree, you are so wrong for this shit!" Tina yelled. He wore a look of embarrassment on his face, but he didn't reply. I was frozen in place. I stood there in shock, trying to come to terms with what I had just seen.

"Are you alright Lex?" Jada asked as she walked over to me. Before I had a chance to answer, I felt that all too familiar feeling in the pit of my stomach. I raced to the back door and pulled it open with my friends hot on my heels. As

144

soon as I stepped out into the yard, I leaned over and released everything that I'd just eaten a few minutes ago.

"Damn, get me some wet towels!" I heard Tyree yelling to someone.

He ran up to me and pulled my hair back out of my face. He held my long curls in one hand, while softly rubbing my back with the other. Jada came back with two cold towels and an ice-cold bottle of water. Tyree stopped rubbing my back and took everything from her. I stood up straight and allowed him to wipe my face and neck with the cold cloth.

"Are you alright baby?" he asked. I took the bottle of water from him without bothering to reply. I tried to walk away, but he pulled be back before I got too far.

"Don't touch me!" I screamed while pulling away from him. I walked back into the house and grabbed my purse. I was so ready to go. I was still feeling a little dizzy, but I would have to manage.

"Alexus, let me talk to you," Tyree begged while walking behind me.

"You feel alright boo?" Tina asked me.

"I'll be alright; I just need to lie down for a while." I lied. I was heartbroken and it was making me physically sick.

"I don't think you should drive. Just go get into one of our beds upstairs," Trina suggested. Any other time, I would have jumped at the chance, but not today.

"No, I just want to go home." My voice cracked but I was determined not to cry, at least not until I made it home.

"You're going upstairs; we need to talk," Tyree said, pulling my hand.

"You can't make her stay if she doesn't want to," Trina said getting in his way.

"Move and mind your damn business." He pushed past her and kept it moving. I must have been moving too slow for him because he turned around and picked me up right before sprinting up the stairs.

"Put me down, I know how to walk," I complained.

We went into the spare bedroom that used to belong to him before he decided to obey my orders. He locked the door and turned to face me before he started to speak.

"I'm sorry about what you saw down there," he said while looking at me.

"You mean, when I saw your girlfriend with your dick shoved down her throat?" My voice was full of sarcasm that I didn't bother trying to hide.

"That is not my girlfriend and you know it."

"Whatever, now I see why we're not together. You still want to be with other people."

"Are you serious right now?" he asked incredulously. "We're not together because of you. You cheated on me and I forgave you because I love you that much. I'm not saying that what I did was right, but don't make it seem like all of this is my fault."

"Why are we even doing this Tyree? It's obvious that we're not meant to be together," I said through tears.

"That is not true. If walking away was that easy, we would have both done that a long time ago."

There was no denying the truth in his words. I didn't want to walk away and, obviously, he didn't either. He walked me over to the bed and helped me get in. When I was settled, he got in behind me in a spooning position and started rubbing my stomach.

"I want us to be together. Like officially, just you and me. I'm willing to do whatever I have to do to make that happen," I said honestly.

"You don't have to do anything. I want the same thing. I love you too much to lose you," he replied while holding me.

146

That was the best news I'd heard in a long time. I hated what I walked in on today, but I couldn't judge him when I was the first one to stray. Right now, I didn't care about Kayla or Dre. If he was willing to forget the past and move on, then so was I. Only time would tell if we were making the right decision. In my heart, I truly believed that we were.

Chapter 18

H urry up and get what the hell you came for and let's go," I told Keanna when we walked up to Troy's apartment.

I didn't want to come but, after she begged my brother Eric and me, we ended up bringing her over here anyway.

Keanna was messy and ratchet as hell, but she was still my family. That nigga, Troy, was dirty for real. After all the shit that he put her through, he ended up putting her out for another bitch. I didn't know Ayanna that well, but I knew for a fact that she was nothing like Alexus. Keanna told me what happened when she walked down on them a few weeks ago, but I wasn't shocked. Troy was a dope fiend and he introduced every woman that he came in contact with to it too. As stupid as Keanna was for him, it shocked me to know that she wasn't strung out by now.

As soon as we walked through the door, the smell hit us before we even got all the way in. Not to mention, the house itself was a mess. Clothes were thrown everywhere; dirty dishes lined the living room table and some parts of the floor. Someone was on the sofa sleeping, but I couldn't make out who it was because the cover was pulled up over their head.

"It stinks in here," Keanna observed while covering her nose.

"Grab you some clothes to last you for a few days and you can come back for the rest later," Eric told her.

"I don't want to leave my stuff here so that crack head bitch can start wearing it."

"Girl, fuck them clothes! You act like that shit was all that. Fill you up a bag or two and let's go!" I yelled in frustration.

We followed her down the hall that led to her bedroom. I knew that Troy's punk ass wasn't gonna be here. Keanna sent him a text when we were on our way. When she told him that we were bringing her over here, his scary ass made up some excuse about having somewhere else to be. Seeing him again was the only reason I really agreed to come in the first place.

I heard music coming from the bedroom, so somebody had to be back there. I put my hand on the gun that rested on my waist just in case I needed to use it. When Keanna opened the door, we saw Ayanna sitting on the floor with her face buried in the coke-lined mirror that she was holding on to. She jumped when she saw us and tried to slide the mirror under the bed.

"No need to hide it now, bitch; we all know how you get down," Keanna said in disgust.

We all looked at her as she pinched the bridge of her nose and held her head back to stop it from bleeding. I walked into the adjoining bathroom and pulled a towel from the rack.

After adding some cold water to it, I went back into the room and threw it to her.

"Damn ma, you might want to lay off that dope," I said, shaking my head.

"I'm fine, don't worry about me," she replied with an attitude.

"Well, fuck you then. Come on and start packing your shit Keanna."

"And make sure you take everything," Ayanna said, standing to her feet.

She was a pretty girl, but I could see the effects that the drugs were having on her already. She'd lost a lot of weight since I last saw her and the dark circles under her eyes made her appear older than she actually was. She had on some short shorts and a tank, but she didn't have enough body to make anyone look twice. She and Lex were definitely night and day in the body area.

"Fuck you!" Keanna said, walking up to her with closed fist.

"Look, I didn't come here for this shit. Get your stuff or I'm leaving your ass here. The fuck is wrong with y'all, fighting over that gay ass dope fiend," I said, stepping in between them.

Keanna looked at me crazy, but she knew better than to say anything. We still weren't on the best terms, so closing her mouth was for the best.

"What's going on in here?" someone asked from the hallway. I heard the footsteps getting closer until Lee peeked in. He looked around the room at all of us, but his eyes lingered on me the longest.

"Hey Dre, how you doing?" He smiled up at me like the girl he wanted to be. Lee was a short, dark-skinned man with short curly hair. Besides the way he dressed, nothing else was masculine about him.

"Don't speak to me. Go sit your feminine ass down somewhere!"

"I was just saying hello. You don't have to act like that." He sounded offended but I didn't give a damn. I was feeling some kind of way about the way he was looking at me. I wasn't Troy and I didn't have a problem showing him the difference between the two of us. He was a drama king in prison and it didn't look like much had changed since he was home.

"That was your first and your last warning before I knock you the fuck out. And you better stop looking at me like that before I slap the piss out of you."

"Alright, I'm sorry. I was just playing with you," he said, holding his hands up in surrender. He was staring at Keanna with a deep scowl on his face before he eventually said something to her.

"Hey Keanna," he said, laughing.

She ignored him and continued to pack her belongings. She had one bag filled and was quickly working on filling another one.

"Ok, I just need to get a garbage bag for my shoes and I'll be ready," Keanna announced.

I was happy to hear that. It felt like I was in a crack house and I was ready to go. I'd been to this house several times in the past, but it'd never looked like this before. Keanna was the one who cleaned and kept up with everything. Since she'd been gone, it was obvious that no one else took her place.

"Are you ready now?" Eric asked Keanna when she came back into the room.

"No, I couldn't find a garbage bag to put my shoes in."

"Well take a few now and come back for the rest later," Eric suggested. He sounded just as aggravated as I did.

"No, I don't want to leave my shoes here. It's bad enough I have to leave some of my clothes."

"Two minutes; that's all the time that you have to grab as many pairs of them cheap ass shoes that you can before you get left behind," I said, getting even more pissed off.

"Ok, just let me grab the ones that I wear the most."

After gathering most of her things, Eric and I carried all of Keanna's bags to my truck and we were on our way.

"Make sure you bring somebody with you when you come back for the rest of your stuff," Eric told her as we drove away.

"I will. Dre, can I ask you a question?"

"What's up?" I countered.

"Who is Lee? When I picked Troy up when he first came home, they were outside of the jail house arguing. Then, when he got in the car, he had an attitude for no reason."

"Oh, he had a reason." Me and Eric laughed but I'm sure the joke went over her head.

"What do you mean by that?"

Either Troy's pimp game was better than I thought or Keanna was really that stupid. All the signs were there, but she still didn't get. I wasn't one to sugarcoat nothing, so I gave it to her raw.

"Y'all are fucking the same man."

"What! You think Troy is messing with Lee?" she asked in shock.

"I don't think, I know he's messing with him. It's been going on since we were in jail. That nigga Troy was foul for even bringing that shit around you though.

"But Lee has a girlfriend," she said, sounding like the naïve fool that she was.

"If you think he have a girlfriend, then you're dumber than I thought you were."

153

"That's fucked up. You knew and didn't even tell me."
She sounded angry but she had me fucked up.

"Girl, I know you didn't just let that come out of your
mouth. You knew that your man was fucking my wife and you
didn't tell me shit. Then, you had the nerve to do a paternity
test on Drew instead of coming to me first. You better be lucky
that I'm even riding your ass around in my truck. And while
we're asking questions, how did you find out about Cherika
and Troy anyway?"

She was silent for a while, but she finally responded.

"I hid a camera in the house and recorded it," she
replied, ashamed.

"Please tell me that you're lying," Eric said, shocked by
her revelation.

"Nope, I got everything on camera." She said that shit
like it was no big deal.

"So, where is the tape now?" I asked.

"It's gone. I was almost tempted to show it to you, but I
changed my mind."

"I don't want to see that shit. It's bad enough that it
happened in the first place."

"So, why didn't you just leave him alone instead of
doing everything that you did?" Eric asked.

"Because I loved him then and I still love him now."

"Well, loving him got you homeless with a broken
heart. You better stop being so naïve," I said.

Keanna was really stupid. No wonder Troy did what he
did to her. A sucker was born every minute and my cousin was
definitely one of them.

Chapter 19

I managed to stay away from Dre for almost two weeks. He was going crazy because I kept my kids away from him too. I was tired of him exposing them to all of his bullshit. I hated how they kept getting put in the middle of all our madness.

First, he introduced them to Alexus and, now, Mya knew who they were. He claimed that he only showed her pictures of them when he was at the facility, but I didn't buy that shit at all. I knew that I was weak for Dre, so the only way that I was able to stay away for so long was because I was staying with my mama. He was blowing my phone up and I knew that he'd probably made several trips to the house looking for me. Well, he was probably looking for the kids more than he was looking for me.

Dre's problem was that he thought he was smart and everybody else was stupid. I'll admit that I was a fool in love for many years, but I was tired of looking stupid for the sake of being married to Dre. I was done listening to his lies. If he couldn't show me that he was serious about us, then I didn't want to hear it. And if that meant keeping my kids away, I was willing to do that too. I didn't give a damn about people saying that I was using my kids to get to him. I was doing what I thought was best.

"When are you going to let these kids see their father? Or at least let them talk to him," my mother said when she entered the kitchen. I was up early making breakfast for everybody.

"I don't know ma. I'm just not for Dre and his drama," I replied.

"I understand you being tired and all, but that has nothing to do with the kids. I'm not Dre's biggest supporter, but I do have to admit that he's good to my grandkids. And you know they love him to death," she said.

I ignored her and cracked some eggs into a bowl. It was crazy that Charde and Cherice were still living with our mother, but they did nothing to help out around the house. They slept until noon and paying a bill wasn't happening. Even when we all lived here at the same time, I was the one who cooked and cleaned when my mama wasn't able to do it. If it wasn't for Dre, I would probably still be living here with them.

That was one of the reasons it was so hard for me to let go. We weren't poor, but I didn't know what living good was until I moved in with him. It was nothing for Dre to give me five grand just for me to go shopping. We spent a lot of time together, even if it was just chilling at home. As far back as I could remember, he'd always cheated, but it didn't get out of hand until he got with Alexus. That's when I felt like I'd lost him for good.

"Are you afraid that you'll give in to him if you see him?" my mother asked, interrupting my thoughts.

"You and I both know that I probably will."

"But you don't have to, Cherika. Millions of people are divorced and the numbers are growing rapidly with each passing day. Mistakes happen. That's why pencils have erasers and ink can be whited out."

The doorbell rang and I was happy for the interruption. Nobody understood how I felt and it was useless for me to keep trying to make them see.

"I'll get it," my mama said, rising from the kitchen table. I continued preparing breakfast until I heard her talking.

"What are you doing here?" She asked someone.

I didn't hear anyone reply, so I kept doing what I was doing. After a few minutes, I heard her close the door.

"Cherika!" she called out to me. When I turned around and saw Dre standing behind her, I almost dropped the pan of biscuits that I was holding.

"Can I talk to you for a minute?" He asked me. The look on my mama's face told me that she wasn't happy, but I was happy that she didn't speak on it.

"I'll finish the food. Y'all can go in the dining room if you want to."

"Thanks ma," I said before walking out of the kitchen, with Dre following close behind.

"What kind of games are you playing?" he asked angrily as soon as I closed the dining room door.

"I'm not the one that's playing games. Do you know how embarrassed I was to run into one of your women with my mama there?"

"I already told you that's not my woman. I've already checked her about that. I don't know what else you want me to do."

"Be faithful, that's all that I've ever asked you to do from day one."

"Man, don't start with that shit again. I'm tired of hearing it."

"And I'm getting tired of saying it!"

"Whatever, where are my kids?"

"They're sleeping."

"That's fucked up how you're keeping them away from me because you're mad." I didn't have a valid reason as to why I kept them away, so I didn't respond.

"What do you have planned for them today?"

"I don't know; I haven't decided yet." The honest answer was nothing. I planned on staying inside today, but he didn't need to know that.

"Well, let me bring them somewhere."

"Where are we going?" I asked, making sure he heard clearly when I said we. He shook his head and laughed at me including myself in his plans. I always did include myself so he should be used to it by now.

"I don't know yet, just have them ready by three," he replied, trying to exclude me. I wasn't having it though.

"We'll be ready."

Later that evening, Dre and I were sitting at the pizza parlor with our kids eating. He picked us up at three just like he said he would, and we all spent the day together. They wanted to go to the aquarium, so that's where we went. I was so happy to finally be having a drama free day with my family. Dre and I were getting along, and the kids were happy. This was how I wanted us to be all the time, so I voiced my opinion to my husband.

"This is how a family is supposed to be," I said while looking over at him. He nodded his head to let me know that he heard me, but he didn't respond.

"So, are you going to let them spend the night with me?" he asked. I wanted to off about him ignoring me, but I refrained.

"No, but you can come spend the night with them."

"That doesn't make any sense. You haven't even been home lately because I've been coming over there every day. That's why I came to your mama's house looking for you." He sounded aggravated but I didn't care.

Him being angry didn't faze me one bit. It was time for me to start calling some of the shots around here.

"Well, if I know that you're coming, then of course I'm going to be there," I replied sassily. We were both silent for a while after that.

"Can we go play the video games?" Lil Dre asked his father.

"Yeah, come on."

Dre looked like he was happy to get up from the table and go play with the kids. They headed from the small game room to the back of the restaurant and started playing the video games. Drew stayed behind and continued to play a race car game on Dre's phone. I had to do a double take to make sure that I was seeing right. Dre never left his phone behind under any circumstances. A great idea came to me, but I had to act fast before Dre came back.

"Don't you wanna go play some of the games in the game room?" I asked Drew.

He looked up at me, but what I said didn't seem to interest him, so he didn't reply. Drew was very nonchalant, so I had to take a different approach with him.

"They have a big motorcycle racing game in the back," I said, trying to convince him.

This seemed to get his attention and he immediately stood up from his chair.

"I want to play the motorcycle game!"

"Go back there and get some quarters from your daddy, so you can play."

He took off running towards the back and joined his brother and sisters in the game room. I wanted to jump for joy when I saw that he left Dre's phone on the table. I hurriedly picked it up before it required me to need the lock code. I wanted to look at his call log and text messages, but I didn't have that much time. Besides, I had an even better idea. I went to the iPhone settings and synced Dre's phone with my iPad. I wouldn't be able to view his calls but, every time he sent or received text messages, I would get it too. I was happy that I decided to bring it with me today to take pictures at the aquarium. I didn't use my iPad very often, but now I wouldn't be caught without it.

Chapter 20

O h shit," I moaned into Alexus' ear. I had her bent over the kitchen sink while I was hitting it from the back. Alexus and I had always had a very active sex life, but it'd been nonstop since she'd been pregnant. Her stomach was in the way, so we were limited on what we could do or at least that was how I felt. I was always worried about hurting her, but she always said that she was alright. She was throwing it back at me like she wasn't three months away from giving birth.

"Baby, slow down; I don't want to hurt you," I said as I tried to slow down her movements.

"Tyree, I'm fine, just keep going," she moaned as she threw it back faster. I'd be lying if I said it didn't feel damn good, but I was nervous at the same time. Alexus was bucking like a horse, and I was having trouble keeping up with her.

"Baby, wait; you're making me nervous."

"Will you just shut up and fuck me!" she yelled in frustration.

She didn't have to tell me twice. As long as she was good, then I was even better. I grab the end of her long ponytail and went all in. I watched her knuckles turn white, as she gripped the edges of the sink even tighter.

"Don't stop!" Lex screamed over and over again, as I pounded into her from behind. I was in my zone and I didn't have any intentions on stopping. After a few more intense minutes, she was screaming again.

"I'm cumming!" Her legs trembled beneath her but I would never let her fall. I held her up by both of her shoulders and braced myself for my release that came soon after. I wanted to collapse on the kitchen floor, but I was holding Alexus up, so I couldn't.

"Damn, the food is burning," Alexus said, pulling away from me.

I forgot all about the food that she was cooking when I first came into the kitchen. I forgot to turn the pots off before I sexually attacked her. Alexus wasn't much of a cook in the beginning, mainly because she didn't know how. During the past few months, with the help of my mother and hers, she'd gotten pretty good. She experimented with lots of different recipes and they always came out good.

"Throw it away, we can eat out," I replied, fixing my clothes.

"That's cool with me."

She did what I told her to do and opened the back door to kill the smell of burning food. I helped her clean up the kitchen before she left to go take her shower. I used that opportunity to give my dad a call. We'd been doing a lot of talking lately, and I valued his advice.

"What happened?" he asked after picking up on the first ring.

"Damn, you must have been waiting on my call."

"Yeah, I was. So, what happened?"

"Nothing yet," I replied.

"Well, why did you call me?"

"I don't know. I'll call you back later."

"Don't call me back unless you have something to tell me," he replied before hanging up.

I went upstairs in search of Alexus and found her in the shower. I stripped out of my clothes and went into the bathroom to join her. My heart was pounding in my chest, but it was now or never. I pulled back the shower curtain and stepped inside. When Alexus looked back at me and smiled, all doubts were removed. I reached my hand in front of her and rubbed her stomach, something that I did quite often.

"Can you see us being in a relationship for a long time?" I asked her.

"Definitely," she replied without hesitation.

"I can't," I said in return. She turned around and looked at me, and I could tell that what I said surprised her.

"Why? What wrong?" she asked in a panicked voice.

The sad expression on her face could not be masked even if she tried. I grabbed her hand and kissed it before replying.

"I want us to have more than just a relationship," I replied as I slipped the ring on her finger.

"Oh, my God! Are you serious?" She gasped in shock, while staring at the seventeen thousand dollar Vera Wang diamond that I'd just placed on her finger.

"I've never been more serious about anything in my life."

After talking to my father about everything that happened with me and Alexus, he helped me to put things into prospective. I laid everything out on the table, including her infidelity with Dre and my mishap with Kayla that she walked in on. He asked me one question that made me see everything clearly. He asked me if I could see myself living without Alexus. If my answer was yes, then I should move on and live my life. If my answer was no, then she was the one and I should make things official. He even made me see the beauty of us going through our storm early, rather than later in our relationship. I now knew that we could overcome anything, no matter what it was.

The paternity of the baby didn't even matter to me anymore. Of course, I wanted him to be mine, but I knew that I would love him regardless of who he belonged to. Once I told my father how I really felt, we went ring shopping the very next day. He thought that I was making the right choice and so did I.

"You don't think we're moving too fast?" she asked nervously.

"No, not unless you're having doubts about us."

"Not at all, this feels right so I know that it is."

"So, can I assume that your answer is yes?"

"No, my answer is hell yes!" she yelled. I pulled her in for a hug and a passionate kiss. The hardest part was over; now, I had something else I needed to run by her.

"I don't know about you, but I don't want to wait. I want us to do something small now and, maybe in a few years once we're established, we can do something bigger."

"So, how soon do you want to do it? I'm free tomorrow."

"Tomorrow," I said, laughing. "We don't even have a marriage license yet."

"You're laughing, but I'm serious," she replied, laughing along with me.

"First, we need to see what all we're going to need and then we can set a date from there."

"That sounds like a plan to me."

Once we were done showering, I called my dad to tell him the good news. My mama and my sisters were happier than I was. They wanted to come over, but he stopped them before they did. They were already making plans and it hadn't even been an hour since we got engaged. When Alexus called to tell her mother, I heard her screaming through the phone, so I knew that she was happy as well. Alexus didn't have a big family like I did, but her mother promised to contact and invite the few that they had.

Two weeks later and it was official. Alexus and I became husband and wife in a poolside ceremony in my parents' massive backyard. Because of my mother and sisters, the wedding ended up being more than we wanted it to be. They bought and decorated an arch for us to stand under, along with an array of fresh flowers that adored each of the tables.

Alexus chose gray and yellow as our colors and they were perfect together. There was enough catered food and drinks to last for a few days thanks to my dad and his brothers. They loved a good party, so they spared no expense. I didn't know it was possible, but they even rented a lighted dance floor for the DJ and guests who really wanted to turn up. Alexus' mother gifted us our four-tier wedding cake, along with the souvenirs that our guests would be taking home with them.

I wore a simple gray linen pants suit, while Alexus wore a long flowing yellow maternity dress. Our day was perfect and I couldn't have asked for a better one. That was why I didn't understand why my new bride was sitting in a lounge chair near the pool looking so sad, while everyone else seemed to be enjoying themselves. I walked over to her and took a seat at the foot of her chair.

"What's wrong baby? I'm surprised you're not tearing up the dance floor with Jada and the twins," I said, laughing.

"I'm good, just thinking about a few things."

"Talk to me, what's on your mind?"

"Even though things are not good with us right now, I still wish that Ayanna was here," she replied sadly.

I found out that after Alexus and I were broken up that her sister, Ayanna, was in on everything with Keanna and Dre. As much as I loved my sisters, I couldn't imagine doing them something so foul. I knew it was hard for her, especially since her other sister and three brothers were here. I'd only met her brother, Alex, so this was my first time meeting everyone else. It was bad enough that my wife's family was small, but they weren't even close. But, she no longer had to worry about that. I had a huge family and we got together every time the opportunity presented itself. They all loved Alexus, so she was welcomed with open arms.

"Where is she?" I asked, referring to Ayanna.

"I don't know. My mama said that she hasn't been around for a few weeks. She used to drop money off for her kids, but that stopped too."

"I understand that you're worried about your sister and all, but this is our wedding day. I don't want you thinking about that and being depressed, especially not today."

Ayanna had done her so wrong, but she still had a lot of love for her. It was written all over her face when she spoke. I didn't want her to be stressed out about anything. This week was going to be our last time being able to relax. Alexus started her clinicals next week and she would be graduating three weeks after that. Then, there was her baby shower and God

166

knows what else in between. We couldn't even take a honeymoon because of everything that was coming up, but she would get one as soon as we were able to go.

"I know, she just runs across my mind from time to time."

"I know she does, but don't worry about it. I'll see what I can find out when this is all over with."

The last I heard from Alexus; her sister was working in a strip club. If it would make my wife happy, I would go over there and ask around to see if I could locate her.

"Thanks baby," she said, smiling.

"So, now that that's settled, let's hit the dance floor."

I helped her up and we made our way to the dance floor right after I refilled my drink. Alexus couldn't drink because of the baby, but I planned to get wasted enough for the both of us. I was genuinely happy and my top priority was making sure that my wife felt the same way.

Chapter 21

I sat in the nail salon getting the finishing touches on my much-needed pedicure. Thanks to my uncle EJ, I had a few extra dollars in my pocket. I was in the process of looking for another job, but I hadn't had any luck yet. I never went back to the club after the incident with Ayanna and Troy. Besides being too embarrassed to face Ayanna, I knew she wanted to pay me back for what I'd done to her.

Besides, she worked at the club long before I came along. Knowing her, she would have probably had me fired anyway. She and Lisa were known for doing that. Lisa's brother was the bouncer and he had a lot of pull with the owner. It didn't matter though because that was water under the bridge since I didn't plan on going back.

Thanks to Troy, I was living with my cousin, Erica, and her mom in the house that belonged to Dre. Eric lived there too when he wanted to lay up with one of his many women. My living arrangements weren't bad, but I was so use to having a place of my own. Even though the apartment we lived in belonged to Troy, I still considered it mine.

I still couldn't believe that he did me dirty like that behind Ayanna's trifling ass. All the years we were together obviously didn't mean anything to him. And, then, there was the conversation with Dre that I couldn't get out of my head. As much as I didn't want to believe it, I knew that it had to be true. Troy had to be having some kind of dealings with Lee. That was the only way to justify his attitude the night they were released from prison. That also explained Troy's attitude towards me when we got home. I went through a lot to give him the perfect homecoming, but I still ended up spending my night alone.

I pulled myself away from my daydream long enough to put on my slippers and head for the door. My phone rang just as I left the nail salon, but I ignored it when I saw a familiar face coming my way.

"Congrats on your soon to be stepchild," I said when Cherika approached the nail salon.

"I swear, New Orleans is too damn small for me. That's exactly why you couldn't keep your man; you're always in somebody else's business," she said while shaking her head.

She looked much better than she did the last time I saw her. But, of course, the last time I saw her, I'd left her in a bloody heap in the parking lot of a store.

"Apparently, he only likes coke whores like you. I'm drug free boo." I smiled smugly.

"Maybe that's why he left you."

"And maybe snorting coke is why Dre left you." I laughed hysterically as I made my way to my car.

"Enjoy your laugh bitch, but I promise I'm going to have the last one!" she yelled.

I gave her the finger in the middle as I backed up and drove away. I was starving, but I didn't want anything that was too heavy. Erica and I were going out to eat later, and I didn't want to ruin my appetite. I decided to get a fruit smoothie to hold me over until later.

When I pulled up to the drive through, I almost changed my mind. There had to be about seven cars ahead of me. I looked through the window of the lobby and only one person was in line. Parking my car, I decided to go in to avoid the long wait. I stood in the lobby, looking over a menu until I was ready to order.

"Hey Keanna," the cashier spoke when I stepped up.

"Hey Tiffany. You look so different."

Tiffany worked as a dancer at the club. She only danced three nights a week, due to her hectic college schedule. Most of the time, she wore long wigs when she danced, but that wasn't the case today. She had on her work uniform and her long ponytail was pulled through the back of her hat.

"Girl, how many jobs do you have?" I asked after I placed my order.

"Only one now; I had to let the club go. It was getting too crazy in there."

"Yeah, I'm not working there no more either."

"I know. I asked about you a few times, but nobody knew where you were. I know you heard about what happened with your friend." She looked at me like she was waiting for an answer.

"If you're talking about Ayanna, I don't fuck with her no more."

"Well girl, apparently, the owner caught her shooting up in the bathroom," Tiffany said, shocking the hell out of me.

I knew that Ayanna snorted coke because I'd see that with my own eyes but shooting up was a horse of a different color.

"Are you serious?" I asked.

"Yep, and then Lisa beat her ass because she stole some of her tip money from her locker," Tiffany continued.

She handed me my smoothie, but I was nowhere near ready to go. Ayanna was wilding out for real. She and Lisa were tight, so I was surprised to hear what was going down between them.

"So, they fired her?"

"I guess so. Some of the other dancers said that Ayanna's boyfriend came back there with a gun. I quit the same night they told me that. That little money is not that serious to me. I'm almost finished with school anyway."

I knew she had to be talking about Troy's stupid ass. If he did have a gun, his scary ass wasn't going to use it.

"I hear that, but she deserves everything that she's getting. Karma is a bitch."

"Well, I'll see you later. I have to get back to work," Tiffany said.

We said our goodbyes and I was on my way. As soon as I got into my car, I called my cousin, Eric. I needed him to come with me to get the rest of my things from Troy's house. If Ayanna was shooting up and stealing, I was pretty sure that he was probably doing the same thing. I didn't want them trying to sell the rest of my stuff before I had a chance to get it.

"Yeah Keanna," Eric said when he answered the phone.

"I need you to come with me to get the rest of my clothes."

"Girl, forget them damn clothes; I'm busy!"

"Please Eric, I need to get the rest of my stuff before they do something with it."

"I can't do it today. I have a lot going on right now," he replied. "Call and ask Dre."

That was out of the question. I was surprised that he came with me the first time.

"Ok," I said before hanging up. I called my cousin, Erica, to see if she was willing to accompany me. To my surprise, she agreed and I was on my way to pick her up.

I didn't know why, but I was nervous when I pulled up to Troy's house. I never knew what to expect, so I had to be careful whenever I came over.

"You need me to come in with you?" Erica asked when I was getting out of the car.

"No, I'm good. I got my protection with me," I said while holding up my Taser.

I grabbed the garbage bags that I'd brought with me and made my way to the front door. I was about to knock, but I decided to use my key instead. After today, I would be leaving it here anyway since I wouldn't have any more use for it.

When I opened the door, the stench almost made me throw up the smoothie I'd just consumed. It almost smelled like the sewer had backed up into the house. I looked around the living room and it was hard to believe that I once called this place home. There were wires hanging in the place of the sixty-inch flat screen that was once mounted on the wall. It didn't take a genius to know that it was probably sold to buy drugs. The leather living room set was also a distant memory, as it had been replaced with a twin-sized blow up mattress. I held my nose as I made my way to the back of the house. Before I got to the bedroom door, I heard talking coming from the other side. I put my hand on my Taser, just as I opened the door. I saw Lee lying across the bed talking on his cellphone.

"Girl, let me call you back. This heifer just walked in here like she's still paying bills," he said to whomever he was talking to. I didn't come for drama, but I was damn sure willing to entertain it if he brought it to me.

173

"Baby, please respect my house. Just because you have a key doesn't mean that you came come and go as you please." His hand rested on his hip just like a bitch.

"I know you don't call this fucking dump a house," I replied with a frown.

"What the hell do you want?"

"I'm coming to get the rest of my stuff. Oh, and you can have this key," I said as I threw the key at him.

"I'm not Ayanna; I will fuck you up in a heartbeat, please believe me."

"I bet your punk ass would. You think you're a woman, that's why you don't mind fighting a real one."

"Troy thinks I'm a woman too. And he definitely fucks me like I am."

"Ugh, let me get my shit and get out of here." I walked over to the closet, preparing to get my stuff and go.

Besides a few hangers and extra blankets, there was nothing else in there. I pulled the blankets out just to be sure, but I still came up empty.

"Where the hell is my shit!" I yelled.

I went to the dresser and opened a few drawers, but they were empty as well. I knew that this was going to happen, which was why I wanted to take everything during the first trip with Eric and Dre.

"They probably sold all my shit to buy drugs!" I screamed.

"I know you better stop making all that damn noise. I saw your stuff, so they probably didn't get too much for it. You basic bitches kill me sometimes."

"Fuck you!" I yelled in frustration.

"It's time for you to go, boo. I don't know what Troy sees in y'all bad built bitches, but I don't have time for this."

"I don't know what he sees in your punk ass," I replied, heated.

"Obviously, something he likes. He left your dumb ass in here alone many nights to be with me, including the day he came home from jail." He smirked but I wanted to die right then and there.

He hit me below the belt with that one. I knew that something was up with Troy, but the thought of him being with Lee never crossed my mind.

"Every dime you sent to that jailhouse was used to make sure I was straight. Every time your car pulled away from the curb, it was me who rode in the front seat. What is it going to take for you and that other dummy to see that he's just not that into y'all?" He laughed.

I'd never felt so small in my life. It was one thing to be cheated on with another woman, but how was I supposed to compete with another man. I didn't know how this got past me for all these years. Troy didn't have a feminine bone in his body, at least none that I'd ever seen. I wondered when it all started and how many other men had there been. I had a million questions running through my head that would probably never get answered. I didn't have a comeback strong enough to dispute what he was saying. Obviously, he knew a side of Troy that I clearly didn't know existed.

"You can have him," I said as I turned to walk away.

"You can't give me something that already belongs to me, boo."

He followed me to the door and held it open like he was waiting for me to leave.

"Oh, and I'll need to get that mailbox key from you as well," he said with his hand extended. He then stood in the doorway like he was preventing me from leaving until he got what he wanted.

"Get out of my way," I said, trying to push past him.

"When you give me what I asked for, I'll be happy to move."

This time, I wasn't gentle when I pushed him and he almost lost his balance.

"Bitch, you must be crazy!" he yelled as he pushed me back just as hard.

I didn't even have time to get my Taser from my pocket before the licks started flying. I couldn't believe his punk ass was actually hitting me. And he didn't hold back when he did. The door closed when we started fighting, so I didn't know if Erica saw us or not. I was trying desperately to hold my balance and keep up, but it was hard. I was looking around the living room for something to defend myself against this wild animal that Lee had become. The living room was a mess, but nothing immediately caught my eye. I was feeling weak and I didn't know how long I could go on. Just then, I looked behind the door and spotted the perfect weapon. Troy didn't live in the best neighborhood, so we always kept a board behind the door to give it extra security when it was locked.

As soon as the opportunity presented itself, I ran over to the door and grabbed it. When Lee came at me again, I swung it hard and caught him at the top of his head. He stopped in his tracks and touched the spot where he was hit. When he looked at his hand, it was covered in blood. He was no longer coming after me, but I swung the board and hit him a second time, just for the hell of it. He pissed me off with the things he said earlier and I was taking that anger out on him now. This time, the board connected with the side of his face. He dropped to his knees and pulled his shirt over his head.

"Bitch, you better run," he said as he wiped away the blood that was streaming down his face.

I dropped the board and opened the door, preparing to do just what he said, run. Erica was still sitting in the car, so I guess she didn't see what was going on. I stepped onto the porch, but I didn't get far before I felt my hair being pulled from behind. I turned around, preparing to swing, but an excruciating pain to my face stopped me. I felt warm liquid pouring from my face as the stinging got worse. I put my hands up to shield my face and, suddenly, they were in pain too.

"Keanna; oh, my God, no!" I heard Erica screaming.

I fell to the ground while Lee stood over me. When he bent down, it was only then that I realized that he was cutting me with something. I saw the silver instrument in his hand, as he crouched down to finish the job. I vaguely heard Erica on the phone calling for help. I was getting weak, so I knew I had to be losing a lot of blood. The pain was so unbearable; I couldn't fight back, even if I wanted to.

"Hey, get the hell away from her!" I heard a male voice scream.

It was only then that Lee stopped his attack on me. He got up and ran away, but not before spitting on me. I couldn't believe that as I laid there on the ground, tasting my own blood in my mouth; he spit on me. I tried very hard to, but I couldn't move. It was like some parts of my body were numb. The only thing that I was able to see was the pool of red blood that I was now lying in.

"Keanna, please don't die on me," Erica cried as she ran over to me. "Help is on the way, just hold on. Please don't die."

"Don't touch her," the man that ran Lee away ordered. As bad as I wanted to keep my eyes open, I couldn't do it. When I closed my eyes, Erica started going crazy.

"Keanna, open your eyes; don't do this to me!"

"Don't worry; her pulse is still very strong. She's probably weak from losing so much blood," the man said.

His voice and the sound of the sirens were the last thing I heard right before I passed out.

Chapter 22

"So, what does that mean?" Tyree asked Dr. Gonzales as he held on to my hand tightly. We were at another one of my doctor's appointment, listening to what the doctor was saying. According to Dr. Gonzales, my baby was in the breech position. It was a possibility that he could turn by the time I gave birth, but there are no guarantees.

"It's no big deal. We deliver breech babies all the time. If he doesn't turn himself around, we'll schedule a date to do a cesarean," Dr. Gonzales said.

I was scared just hearing that word. Ayanna had a C-section with her last two kids. She was in so much pain that my mother had to take care of the babies for her. She cried for days and the medicine that she was prescribed didn't seem to help much.

"So, there's still a possibility for me to have him naturally?" I asked, feeling hopeful.

"There is, but I would much rather you have a C-section, whether he turns around or not. You have a very small frame, but you're carrying a rather big baby. You're only seven months and he's already about six pounds with two more months of growing to go."

"So, how big do you think he's going to be?" Tyree asked curiously.

"If I had to guess, I would say between nine to eleven pounds."

"What!" I yelled in shock. My stomach was big, but it wasn't that big to be having a monster growing inside of me.

"Calm down baby." Tyree squeezed my hand trying to comfort me. That was easy for him to say since he wouldn't be the one being torn apart by a gigantic baby.

"It sounds worse than it actually is. Trust me, it'll be well worth it when you see your baby for the first time." Dr, Gonzales smiled at me reassuringly. That may have been true, but I wasn't thinking about that right now.

When we finished up with the doctor, I got my appointment for the following month. I would soon be coming in for visits once a week, instead of once a month. His arrival was getting closer and I was getting more nervous as the days passed.

"I have about an hour before my meeting. You want to get something to eat before you go to the hospital?" Tyree asked me.

I was a week into my clinical training at West Jefferson Medical Center and I loved it already. I had about two weeks left and, then, it would be time for me to graduate. My baby shower was scheduled for one week after graduation and, then, I would be able rest until my baby was born. I had a lot on my plate, but it was all going to pay off in the end.

"Yeah, I have some free time to kill before I have to be there," I said while staring off into space.

"What's wrong baby?"

"I'm scared." I know I sounded childish but it was the truth.

"It's just fear of the unknown, you'll be alright," he said nonchalantly.

"Did you not just hear her say that I was going to be giving birth to the Incredible Hulk? I don't even see how something that big can come out of me."

"I know you're scared, but you know I'll be right there the whole time," he said, squeezing my hand.

I was so blessed to not only have Tyree in my life, but to have him as my husband. He might not have been perfect, but he was perfect for me. I couldn't have asked for a better man and I was proud to carry his last name.

"I know baby and I appreciate you." I leaned over and gave him a kiss.

"So, what do you feel like eating?"

"It doesn't matter, as long as I can get it to go. I want to stop by my mama before I go to the hospital."

We ended up going to a sandwich spot not far from the clinic. We ate in the car0 while we talked about our upcoming bundle of joy. Tyree was scared of spoiling him too much, but I was scared of something else. As happy as Tyree and I were right now, I knew that could all change once the baby was born. Dre was going to make our lives miserable if this baby was his. I didn't think he knew that we were married yet, but it was only going to get worse once he found out.

"You want me drop you off by your mama?" Tyree asked, once we were done eating.

"No, you can bring me home to get my car. That's going too far out of your way. Besides, you're making me way too lazy," I replied with a smile.

I hated driving and everybody knew it, especially Tyree. He waited on me hand and foot. I never had to drive if he was free. Today would be my first time driving myself in over a month.

I called my mother to make sure she was home before I just dropped in on her. As soon as I was given the green light, I was on my way over. I hadn't seen her and the kids in a few days and I looked forward to spending a little time with them.

When I turned on her street, I had to do a double take when I saw Ayanna's car parked out front. The car started to slowly pull away from the curb and she appeared to be leaving. I blew my horn to stop her before she did. The car stopped just as I pulled up in the driveway. I wobbled out of my car and stood next to the driver's side door, waiting for Ayanna to get out. I thought she would get out of the driver's side, but she exited the passenger's side instead.

Since her windows were heavily tinted, I couldn't tell who was behind the wheel. When she walked from behind the car, I wanted to cry at the sight that stood before me. Ayanna was always thin but, now, she was nothing but sticks and bones. Her cheeks were sunken and her hair was nappy and matted on top of her head. She was fidgeting nervously as she came closer to where I stood. There was no denying that she was on drugs.

"Mama told me that you were pregnant, but I didn't know you were that big," she said awkwardly.

The musty stench that came from her body and clothes almost made me throw up, but I kept my composure.

"Yeah, it'll be over in about two months," I replied. I looked down at the track marks and sores that covered her arms and I wanted to cry.

"I know we haven't talked in a while, but are you okay?" I asked.

182

It was a stupid question because I knew that she wasn't okay, just by looking at her. I was just trying to make small talk since I didn't have anything else to say.

"Yeah, I'm fine. I just came to see mama and my kids, but that wasn't such a good idea."

"Why, what happened?"

"You know how she is; she's worried about nothing."

"No she's not, Ayanna. You're on drugs and that's why she's worried."

"Yeah, I was, but not anymore. I'm getting myself together."

I didn't get a chance to respond before the driver's side window came down on her car. I almost died when Troy stuck his scrawny neck out of the window and started yelling.

"Let's go Ayanna. I got moves to make!" he hollered.

"Ayanna, no; please tell me that you are not with Troy."

"Yeah, we're together," she replied nervously.

This was worse than I thought. *If she's with Troy, then where in the hell is Keanna?* I thought to myself.

"Ayanna, he is not right. You need to leave him alone. You know that mama will let you move back home if you get yourself cleaned up."

"Don't do that okay? I know that you don't like him, but he's good to me, Lex," she said, defending that bastard.

"How is he good to you, Ayanna? You're filthy and your hair is a mess."

"Ayanna, I said let's go!" Troy yelled again while honking the horn.

"I have to go. Uh, Lex, do you think you can lend me a few dollars? I'm hungry," she said while rubbing her stomach.

"Why didn't you go inside and eat something?"

"Because… I don't know, I just didn't. Can you just give me a little something please?"

I reached into my purse and pulled out a twenty-dollar bill. When I handed it to her, the look on her face said it all. Her eyes lit up like a Christmas tree. I'd just provided the resources for her to get her next hit.

"Thanks sis," she said excitedly, as she pulled me in to hug her funky body. I had to hold my nose to keep from throwing up.

"I love you, Lex," she said right before she got into the car. I didn't doubt her love for me, but I knew that she loved the twenty I'd just given her even more.

"Please tell me that you didn't just give her money," my mama said, appearing in the doorway.

She probably saw me, so there was no need to lie. I put my head down without giving her an answer, but she already knew.

"Alexus, don't give her any money. You know she's just going to buy more drugs with it," she scolded.

"I'm sorry; I just felt so sorry for her," I said sadly. A part of me felt guilty about how everything went down between Ayanna and me. If she wouldn't have gotten put out of my mama's house, she wouldn't have ended up with Troy's crazy ass. True, she did me wrong but I hated to see her in the condition that she was in.

About an hour later, I was pulling up to the hospital. I spent a little time with my mother before it was time for me to be here. I wasn't in on the planning of my baby shower, but she was going on and on about how nice it was going to be. My in-laws were going all out according to what she was saying. I didn't want it to be a surprise, so I already knew when and where it was going to be.

"Hey Mrs. Peterson," I spoke when I went into the break room. I put my purse in the temporary assigned locker and took a seat next to her.

"Hey baby," Mrs. Peterson spoke back. She was also a physical therapy assistant but, unlike me, she'd been on the job for almost thirty years. She was the one who had been training me for the past week.

"We have a light day today. Two of our patients went home so that only leaves us with three. We got two in the burn unit and the other one just got transferred in last night. I haven't had a chance to see them yet."

Our job was to assist patients with movement dysfunction that may result from diseases, disorders, conditions, or injuries. Once I graduated, I planned to work at a clinic rather than a hospital. That way, I would still have my nights and weekends free to spend time with my son and husband.

"I'm ready whenever you are," I replied enthusiastically. I was excited to be actually getting some hands-on training and I wanted to learn everything that I could.

"Good evening," a short, petite lady said when she walked into the break room.

"Well, look who finally decided to come back from vacation," Mrs. Peterson said as she stood up and gave the woman a hug.

"And I'm happy to be back," the woman replied, smiling. Something about her looked familiar, but I couldn't figure out where I knew her from.

"Alexus, this is Brenda. She's been a registered nurse here for almost twenty-five years," Mrs. Peterson said as she introduced us.

"Alexus is doing her clinical training here. She'll be graduating in two weeks," Mrs. Peterson continued while smiling at me.

The other lady looked at me like she, too, was trying to remember where she knew me from. She smiled sweetly and reached her hand out and grabbed mine.

"It's nice to meet you, Alexus. I see you have a lot going on besides graduation," she said, rubbing my stomach.

"Yeah, and she just got married," Mrs. Peterson replied excitedly.

"Well, congratulations to you on everything," Brenda said as she continued to hold my hand and smile.

I couldn't explain it, but I got a good vibe from her. She seemed so genuine when she spoke.

"Thank you," I said, smiling in return.

"We better get started Alexus. We have a patient on your floor, so we'll be seeing you, Brenda," Mrs. Peterson said.

Over the course of the next two hours, Mrs. Peterson and I saw the two patients on the burn unit. They were siblings who were burned in a house fire that was set by their father. It was a blessing that they weren't burned too badly, but they had trouble moving their limbs as well as they did before. Mrs. Peterson stood by and watched while I assisted them with their daily exercise routine. They both seemed to be getting better since I started helping them a week ago.

"Here's the chart for the last patient. She's on the fifth floor. I have to assist with something else, so you can get started on her if you want to. I'll be up as soon as I'm done." Mrs. Peterson handed me a clipboard with the patient's information.

"Ok, thanks," I replied before catching the elevator to the fifth floor.

Before going into the room, I always liked to read the patient's chart to see what was going on with them.

"What the hell!" I said out loud to no one in particular.

I read the name on the chart over and over, but it still read the same way. I used the wall to hold me up as I read over the chart with the name, Keanna Mack, at the top of it. According to Keanna's chart, she had been cut repeatedly with a sharp object. Her hands showed signs of defensive wounds and she had trouble moving them around, which was why she required physical therapy. My mind then wandered to my sister. I wondered if she was somehow responsible for the attack on Keanna since she was now with Troy. I closed my eyes and prayed that I was wrong.

"Small world huh?" I heard someone say.

I looked up into the smiling face of Brenda. I didn't have to ask what she was talking about because she went on to tell me.

"It took me a minute, but I was finally able to put two and two together," she said.

"Huh?" I asked with a confused expression on my face.

"I'm talking about Keanna. She and my daughter used to be friends."

Now, I was really confused as to whom she was, as well as who her daughter was.

"I'm Cherika's mother," she said, looking at me for a reaction. Unfortunately, I didn't have one. But, now, I knew why she looked so familiar to me. We'd never met, but Cherika looked just like her.

"Wow," was all I managed to say.

"I know the feeling."

"This is all too much."

187

"Yes, it is, but I see that you're moving in the right direction and that's away from Dre. I've been praying that my daughter can do the same thing one day."

"That was one mistake that I wish I could take back," I replied honestly.

"I understand. You are a beautiful girl and, judging by the ring on your finger, you have a man that loves you. Dre didn't deserve you and he doesn't deserve my daughter. She just doesn't realize it yet."

"Well, I had to learn the hard way. Nothing and nobody is worth me losing my husband."

"I know that's right. Listen, I know that you have to go and so do I, but would it be alright if I prayed with you?"

"Yes, please do."

Prayer was something that I could never have enough of. I closed my eyes and lowered my head as Brenda held my hand and prayed for me. She also prayed for my marriage and the health of my unborn baby. When she was done, she gave me a tight hug before walking away. I couldn't believe how sweet she was. After all, I was her daughter's husband's mistress at one time, but none of that seemed to matter to her. I really needed that and I felt so much better afterwards.

Walking slowly, I made my way down the hall to Keanna's room. The last time I saw her was outside of the club when I beat her down. So much had happened since then. I paused outside of her door to calm my nerves. It wasn't that I was scared to see her; I just didn't know what I was going to see. I took a deep breath, turned the knob on the door, and slowly walked in while knocking lightly.

"Keanna," I softly called out to her. She had her back to me, so I didn't see her injuries yet. I didn't know if she heard me the first time, so I called her name again. This time, she stirred in the bed and turned her body to face me.

That was something that I wished she had not done. Pregnant or not, the sight of her would make anyone vomit.

Her face was covered in staples that I knew were going to be scars once they came out. She even had staples on the side of her head where her hair was shaved to operate. She was extremely swollen and almost unrecognizable.

"Alexus?" she asked, shocked by my presence.

"Yeah, it's me."

"What are you doing here?"

After telling her why I was there, I asked her some questions in order to fill out the necessary paperwork for the night shift employees.

"I'm supposed to help you exercise your hands. If it hurts too much, just let me know and I'll stop."

As grossed out as I was, I still had a job to do. I put on some gloves and softly grabbed one of her hands. I tried not to look at her face but, when she started talking, I really had no choice.

"Your stomach is huge," she said, laughing.

"Yeah, I know," I laughed with her.

"Do you know what you're having?"

"It's a boy."

She looked uncomfortable, so I wanted to make sure that she was alright.

"Are you in pain?" I asked her.

"No, they numbed me up pretty good. I really can't feel anything."

We were quiet for a while until she started talking again.

"You probably don't want to hear this, but I just want to apologize for everything that I did to you," she said, surprising me.

I never thought I'd hear those words come from her mouth, but they were welcomed. My mother always said that apologizing was one of the hardest things to do and acceptance was sometimes harder. I didn't feel that way though.

"I accept your apology, but can I ask you something?" She nodded her head telling me yes.

"Why did you do it? I mean, we were friends or at least I thought we were at one time."

"Jealousy," was her one word answer. "I liked Tyree and I was mad when I found out that y'all were together. I know it's stupid, but it's the truth. I'm sorry that I'm the cause of y'all not being together."

"Who said that we're not together?" I asked while holding up my wedding ring for her to see. Even though she just apologized, I still saw the jealously in her eyes as she stared at my finger.

"Y'all got married?" she asked with a hint of anger in her voice.

"We sure did."

"Does Dre know?"

"No, but I'm sure you'll tell him," I replied sarcastically.

"No, I won't; I promise."

"I really don't care if you do. It won't change anything."

We went back to being silent while I continued to work on her hands. I wanted to ask her what happened, but I never got the chance. Mrs. Peterson came into the room followed by two other gentlemen and her supervisor. She had a look of fear on her face and I soon found out why.

"Alexus, I need you to step over here for a minute," Mrs. Peterson said nervously.

I stood up and looked around at everyone before doing as I was told. The two men walked over to Keanna's bed.

"Are you Keanna Mack?" one of the men asked.

"Yeah," Keanna replied nervously.

"I'm Detective Warren and this is Detective Raymond. We have a warrant for you arrest!"

"A warrant for what!" Keanna yelled.

"You're under arrest for battery and feticide against Cherika Mack. As of right now, you are in the custody of the Orleans Parish Prison. We'll have a guard outside your door until you are released from the hospital and taken into custody," Detective Warren said right before he read Keanna her rights.

My mouth hung wide open when he told her what she was under arrest for. I remembered Dre telling me that Cherika had a miscarriage, but he never told me how.

"That's bullshit; it's my word against hers and she's lying!"

"Well, we have a witness that identified you at the scene, along with a sworn statement from the victim. Don't worry; you'll have your day in court to tell your side of the story," Detective Raymond said.

He must have had her right because she didn't have a response to his last statement. The detectives spoke with the floor supervisor and the head of hospital security about what they could and could not do as far as Keanna's visits and privileges. Her hands were cut up pretty badly, so they decided not to cuff her to the bed. She was sobbing uncontrollably as the detectives continued to talk.

"I need to call my family," Keanna cried.

"You'll still have access to the phone," one of the gentleman told her.

Even though she'd done me wrong on several occasions, I felt bad for her as the tears poured from her eyes. Leaving Dre and his entire family alone was one of the best decisions I could have ever made. There's no telling what kind of drama I would be mixed up in if I didn't.

As soon as I was cleared to leave, I rushed out of the room to call my husband. He was just as shocked as I was about everything that I told him. After seeing what happened to Keanna, I was even more thankful to have him in my life.

Chapter 23

"**B**oy, you better slow down!" my pops yelled as I sped across the bridge.

"I'm trying to catch somebody at the house while it's still early," I replied, slowing down slightly.

It was almost ten in the morning and we were on our way to Troy's house. It was no secret that I was in a hurry to get there. When we got the call from Erica saying that Keanna had been stabbed, I was shocked to find out that Lee was behind the attack.

My first thought was that Ayanna was the one who was responsible. My cousin and I didn't have the best relationship, but she didn't deserve that. This was going to be our third time coming over here, but nobody was ever home when we came. It didn't matter if I ran into Troy or Lee because I wanted both of them.

In my opinion, Troy was just as guilty as Lee was since he was the one who invited him into their relationship. Erica said that a man who was walking his dog was probably the only reason why Keanna was alive. The man saw what was happening and rushed over to help. Lee ran off right after and hadn't been seen since.

When we first went to the hospital to visit Keanna, we couldn't even tell who she was. Her face was swollen and bandages covered everything but her eyes. She slept most of the time because of the pain medicine that she was being fed all throughout the day. She'd recently been moved to another hospital, but I hadn't seen her since she got there. My sister, Erica, told me that she was going to have some nasty scars on her face and hands whenever her staples and stiches were removed.

"I doubt if he'll come back to the house after what he did," Eric said from the back seat.

"You never know, some people are just that dumb," I replied as we pulled up to Troy's apartment. I got excited when I saw that the door was partially opened. Eric and I jumped out at the same time and made our way up to the front door. When we opened the door, my mouth hung open in shock. There was nothing in there that even indicated that the place was once occupied. Two men were in the living room pulling up what was left of the carpet, while another one was painting the wall in the hallway.

"Can I help you?" one of the men asked, looking at us strangely.

"What happened to the people who use to live here?" I asked.

"I really don't know. We're contracted through the complex to get the apartments cleaned up after a move out."

"Well, what happened to all the furniture and stuff that was in here?" Eric asked him.

"They didn't have much of anything in here. We threw out the few blankets and clothes that were left behind. Most likely, they were evicted for non-payment of rent. That's what the case is most of the time."

"Alright, thank you," I said before leaving.

"Well, that's a lost cause. It's no telling where they're living at now," Eric said.

We got in the truck and relayed the information to my pops. He seemed to be just as pissed as we were, but it was more personal for him. He'd been like a father to Keanna since his brother died, so he took it harder than the rest of us. He never did like Troy and this only added fuel to the fire.

"You don't think he can be staying with some of his friends or family?" my pops asked me.

"I seriously doubt that. He don't really talk to none of his family and I don't think he have too many friends."

Troy has a big family, but none of them wanted to deal with him for some reason. He claimed that it was because he sold drugs but, now that I think about it, it was probably because he was using them.

"What about Alexus' sister? You think he might be living with her?"

"Hell no, Anita don't play that shit. I know for a fact that he's not living over there."

"Hello," my pops said, answering his phone. "What! I'll be over there in a little while."

"What happened?" Eric and I asked at the same time.

"Erica said that they arrested Keanna at the hospital. When she gets released, she's going straight to jail." He almost looked like he was in shock when he answered.

"What! She's the one who got attacked. Why is she going to jail?" I was just as shocked and confused as he was.

"Erica said they arrested her for battery and feticide."

"I know what battery is, but what the hell is feticide?" Eric asked before I could.

My pops looked over at me before he answered the question.

"They said that she was the one who made Cherika lose her baby," he replied, surprising the hell out of me.

I knew that Cherika was lying about what happened when she had the miscarriage, but I never thought that Keanna had anything to do with it. I had some questions and she had a lot of explaining to do.

Chapter 24

It was almost noon when I was awakened by the excessive ringing of my doorbell. I had a massive headache that I just wanted to sleep away. My children were with my mother and I'd been home drinking all night. She had to be at work at two, so I figured she was bringing them home before she left.

"I'm coming!" I yelled, dragging myself from my spot on the sofa.

That was where I spent most of my nights whenever I was home alone. Unfortunately, that was most of the time. Without checking to see who it was, I unlocked the door and walked away. I expected my kids to come rushing inside, but it was their no-good ass father who entered instead.

"You're fucking pathetic," he said, picking up the bottle of peach Cîroc that I'd emptied the night before.

I was in such a hurry to open the door that I'd forgotten to clean up the pile of empty bottles that littered the floor. I hated myself for starting to drink again, but I had a lot on my mind. Alcohol was a way for me to temporarily forget about all of my problems. Unfortunately, the problems would still be there once the alcohol wore off and I would feel even worse.

"What are you doing here?" I asked as I looked into his angry face.

He looked around my living room at the mess that I'd been living in for the past few days and turned up his nose in disgust.

"What you did was really fucked up, Cherika. I don't understand why it took so long for you to say something if that's what really happened between you and Keanna. You wait until the damn girl is laying up in a hospital bed for you to send the police at her!"

"So, I'm wrong for wanting to see the person that caused me to lose our child punished? I don't give a damn where she was!"

"That shit happened a year ago!"

"So, and what's your point?" I asked flippantly.

"I asked you to tell me the truth about how you lost your baby and you sat in my face and lied."

"Our baby!" I yelled in frustration. "I'm tired of everybody saying my baby all the time."

"That shit is irrelevant. I don't give a damn who the baby was for," he said, hurting my feelings.

"It was for your dog ass!"

"Yeah, just like Drew."

"Fuck you!" I yelled as the tears started falling.

"I'm happy that we didn't get back together. Your ass is crazy for real."

"If I'm crazy, it's because you made me this way."

"What's going on in here? I heard y'all before I even got out of my truck," my mama said as she pushed my front door open.

"Nothing, I'm leaving," Dre said, walking towards the door.

Of course, my kids weren't going to let him leave without a fight. They were begging to go with him, but I wasn't having it. I didn't want him or his whores anywhere around my babies.

"I'm taking them with me for a little while," he announced.

"No, you're not; they just got home."

We went back and forth arguing until my mother had to intervene. She pulled me to the side and went off on me.

"You need to stop this. Judging from all these empty liquor bottles, you are in no position to care for them. I can still smell it on your breath. Let them spend some time with their father until you sober up," she whispered harshly.

"They can only stay until tomorrow," I conceded, after the truth in my mother's words sunk in.

She was right. I had a terrible hangover and my head was pounding like a drum. The only thing I was going to do was make them go into their rooms while I went back to sleep.

Dre took the kids and left, but my mother stayed behind.

"I don't know what's going on with you and I really don't care. I'm tired of trying to help you and you keep refusing it. But, I won't sit by and watch you ruin my grandkids. If you need me to take them for a little while until you get yourself together, just let me know."

"I'm fine and my kids are fine right here with me."

"I doubt that very seriously. You let that man drive you crazy. I've tried everything that I can think of to help you, but I don't know what else to do except keep you in my prayers."

"Like I just said, I'm fine."

I started picking up the empty bottles that were scattered all over the floor. I felt my mother watching me, but I refused to acknowledge her glare.

"You can keep lying to yourself if you want to, but you need help. I feel so sorry for those babies."

"Don't worry about my kids!" I yelled angrily.

"I'm trying to do the right thing by asking you. Please don't make me get the courts involved because you know I will for the safety of my grandkids," she threatened.

"Nobody is taking my kids away from me." I got defensive and I had every right to do so.

"Well, you better stop giving me reasons to want to take them," she replied, before walking out the door.

I locked the door behind her and used it to hold me up as I dropped down to the floor in tears. Everybody was against me, even my own mother. I couldn't believe that she threatened to take my kids away from me.

Maybe Dre was right, maybe I was crazy, but he drove me to it. All he had to do was be honest with me, but he couldn't even do that. He kept telling me that he wanted to work things out, but that was a lie from the start. I saw every text that came through on his phone, including the ones that he sent.

Mya wasn't the only female that I had to worry about. In fact, there were a whole lot more than just her. He texted Alexus the most, but she rarely replied. She always gave him generic one word answers when she did. I only knew that it was her because they only talked about the baby. Whenever he told her that he loved her, she didn't answer or she threatened to block him from texting her altogether.

Honestly, I didn't recognize any of the numbers because they weren't saved in my iPad, but I could tell the ones that were from Mya.

Keanna was staying with my mother-in-law and, apparently, she and Mya met when she went over there with Dre one day. I guess they started hanging out because some of her texts would say that she was with Keanna when Dre inquired.

That was the last straw with me, as far as Keanna was concerned. That was her last time crossing me and I made sure of it. I contacted the detective that was over my case and decided to move forward with it. They even went back to the store and spoke to the clerk who saw us fighting in the parking lot that night. When they showed him Keanna's picture in a lineup, he was able to identify her at first glance. That and the cameras that hung outside of the store was enough for them to get a warrant for her arrest.

I tried calling Erica, but she never answered for me. Even when I talked to my mother-in-law, she had an attitude like she didn't want to be bothered, so I left her alone too. With the way I was feeling, they could get it too.

I was sick and tired of letting everybody walk all over me, especially my husband. Since everybody thought I was so crazy, it was time for me to show them just how crazy I could be.

Tyree

Chapter 25

It was my wife's graduation day and I was probably more excited than she was. My family and some of hers made up the first two rows of the perfectly manicured lawn that our chairs rested on. When they called Lex's name to receive her degree, I stood up in the chair and went crazy, right along with the rest of my family. I was so proud of her and I wanted the world to know it. Being eight months pregnant and graduating with the fourth highest GPA in your class wasn't easy, but she did it. I knew I was the loudest one out there, but I didn't give a damn.

"Tyree, sit down before you get us put out of here," my mama said while grabbing my pants leg.

"I'm not worrying about these people. I'm cheering for my wife," I said while taking my seat. Jada and my sisters were just as loud as me. They had whistles and all kinds of noise makers with them.

Aside from them handing out degrees, everything else about graduation was boring to me. I sat there through another hour of talking before they finally started wrapping things up. Once it was over, I pushed my way through the crowd until I found my wife.

"Congratulations baby, I'm so proud of you," I said, pulling her in for a big hug.

"Thanks boo. I'm happy that it's over."

We walked hand in hand until we joined the rest of our family. After everybody exchanged hugs and well wishes, we were ready to leave. I wanted to give Lex a graduation party, but my mama talked me out of it. Her baby shower was only a few days away, so she felt like that would have been too much work. Instead, I rented the banquet room of a restaurant and we celebrated with food and drinks. Jada and my sisters provided the graduation cake that rested in the center of the table. I was so happy that all of this would be over soon. I knew that Lex was tired and I just wanted her to get some rest until the baby came.

"Am I finally going to see the nursery today?" Lex asked as I sat another plate of food in front of her.

She was definitely eating for two, judging by the amount of food she'd consumed so far. She was also driving me crazy about seeing what my pops and I had done with the baby's room so far. It took a while for me to convince her to let me have total control over decorating the nursery, but she finally did. She wanted to do the Mickey Mouse theme, but I wasn't having it.

"I told you that you can see it after the baby shower."

"That's not fair that everybody's seen it except me. She pouted and almost made me feel bad.

"That's because they've been helping me put everything together."

She was nosey as hell, so I had to keep the door locked at all times. I knew that she was going to love it and I couldn't wait for her to see it.

For the next few hours, we sat around and enjoyed spending time with our friends and family. When all the food and cake was gone, we all went our separate ways.

Five days later, we were preparing the hall for Alexus' baby shower. I didn't know too much about decorating, but my mama had the place looking like a page from a book. The entire room was decorated in light blue, brown, and white. In the front entrance was a huge portrait of me and Alexus that was taken a few weeks ago, with the word 'Congratulations' written at the bottom of it.

Alexus had already gotten her hair and nails done, so all she had to do was get dressed and wait for me to pick her up. Jada and my sisters were already here, making sure that everything was straight. We didn't have to worry about food because that was being catered and served as well. My mama had also hired somebody to do a dessert table with all kinds of candy and sweets. There were two huge chairs that faced the guests that Alexus and I would be sitting in.

"You better go home and get dressed. There's nothing left for you to do here. People are going to start arriving soon," my mother said, walking up to me.

"I know; I'm about to leave. Alexus is going to kill me if we're late."

I pulled my keys out of my front pocket and prepared to leave. I took one last look around the hall before making my way to the exit. We had about an hour before it was time for us to return. I needed to take a shower and get dressed in that amount of time.

When I walked into the house, Alexus almost knocked me down as she rushed up to me and gave me a big hug.

"Baby, it's so pretty," she gushed while shoving her phone in my face.

I was pissed when I looked at the pictures of the baby shower that Jada and my sisters had posted on Facebook and Instagram. Alexus didn't have to rush to see any of it because it was all over the internet.

"They are so stupid. I can't believe they put the shit on the computer, knowing that you would see it," I said angrily.

Those dummies had the entire invitation posted online. It was reasons like this that had me really starting to hate social media.

"I'm not going to say anything. I didn't even like or comment on any of it, so they don't know that I saw it."

"That's not the point. That was a stupid move they made."

"I shouldn't have even told you that I saw it grumpy. Go get dressed, so we can go," she said, walking away.

When I got upstairs and saw the clothes that she was planning to wear, we had another problem that had to be dealt with.

"Is this what you're wearing?" I asked with a frown.

I didn't have a problem with the outfit because I'd helped her pick it out. My problem was with the heels that she planned to wear with it.

"Yes, it's the same outfit that we picked out last week."

"I'm not talking about the outfit; I'm talking about these heels. What happened to the flats that we picked out to go with it?"

"That's for me to change into if I'm tired of the heels."

"Hell no! You are not wearing any heels at eight months pregnant!"

"But, it's a wedge heel. They're comfortable and I can walk in them fine."

"I don't care; the answer is still no," I said with finality.

I wasn't surprised when the tears started. For the past few weeks, any and every little thing made her cry. My mama told me that it was because her hormones were off balance. I didn't know what the hell it was, but I was ready for it to be over with. The pitiful look on her face when she cried was enough to make me cry too.

"Baby, don't cry; I'm sorry," I said as I pulled her in for a hug. "Listen, I have an idea. How about you walk in with the heels on and you can change into your flats after you finish taking pictures? Just please stop crying."

"Okay," she nodded, still crying. I guess that wasn't good enough, but I didn't know what else to do. Then, suddenly, a great idea came to mind that I knew would cheer her right up.

"I'll let you see the nursery right now if you stop crying."

"Alright." She hurriedly wiped her face and the tears stopped just as fast as they started.

"Well damn." I laughed at how fast she regained her composure.

She was smiling hard when I put the key in the door knob and turned it. It didn't even look like she was crying a minute ago.

"Oh, my God!" She screamed in amazement when I opened the door and walked her in.

"You like it?" I asked, even though the look on her face told me she did.

"Yes, I love it," she replied as the tears started up again.

With the help of both of our mothers, I decided on the king of the jungle theme for the room. The colors stood out and the title was perfect for the soon to be new addition to our family. My mama insisted on Lex having a rocking chair, so that was placed against the wall near the window. I wanted his name to go on the wall, but we weren't sure what his name was going to be. Of course, if he was mine, he was going to have my father's and my name. I wanted him to have my name, even if he wasn't mine, but Dre's punk ass was going to make that almost impossible.

"I'm going to take my shower while you look around. We need to get going in a minute," I said, walking out of the room.

Thirty minutes later, we were walking into the hall full of baby shower guests. When I left a little while ago, there was no one here. Now, every table in the room was filled. The table that held the gifts was filled to capacity with more gifts lining the floor around it.

"Where in the hell are we going to put all of this stuff?" I whispered to Lex while we sat up front in our chairs.

"I was just thinking the exact same thing," she whispered back.

There was no way in hell that we would be able to open all these gifts today, on top of opening over one hundred envelopes that held cash or gift cards. It was going to take several trips or several cars for us just to get it all to our house.

"I see your sneaky ass is still wearing those heels."

I observed Lex when she returned to her seat. She'd been walking around for over an hour talking to everybody, but she had yet to put her flats on. Sometimes, I didn't know why I even bothered when I knew I was going to give in to her anyway.

"You don't miss nothing." She laughed but I wasn't playing with her.

Before I could reply, I looked up and saw Jada and my sisters rushing over to us, looking scared and panicked.

"We have a problem," Jada said to Alexus and me.

"What's wrong?" The look on Jada's face said a lot. Something was definitely wrong.

"Dre is outside. He's acting a fool because no one will let him in to bring his gift."

"What! How the hell did he even know about the baby shower?"

"He's going to ruin everything," Alexus said as she started crying for the hundredth time today.

"No, he's not, just calm down baby," I told Lex while grabbing her hand.

"I don't know how he found out," Jada spoke up.

"Everybody and their mama probably know since y'all posted the shit all over the internet," I said to her and my sisters.

"What's going on?" my mama asked as she rushed to Alexus' side, along with my father.

"Alexus' ex-boyfriend is outside," Jada said.

"That nigga must be crazy showing up here. He got my daughter-in-law all upset and shit," my pops said, going off.

I stood up just as he motioned for his brothers to come over.

"Y'all don't leave out of here. Let the paid security handle that," my mama told us. The hall we rented came with two paid police officers, but I really didn't care about them.

When I got close to the exit, I heard the commotion before I saw anybody. I heard the police telling somebody that they needed to leave, but I couldn't hear what the reply was.

When I walked out the door, I saw Dre and another man standing there talking to the police. When he looked up and saw me, the hate was written all over his face. He started walking in my direction, followed by the man that he came with. Maybe he thought he intimidated me, but he really had the wrong nigga. It was one thing when Alexus was my girlfriend, but it was a whole different ball game now that she was my wife.

Chapter 26

When I looked up and saw Alexus' punk ass boyfriend come outside, I had fire in my eyes as I walked over to him. I didn't think I'd ever hated anybody the way I hated that clown. It pissed me off to think that this nigga just came out of nowhere and thought he had it like that.

"What the fuck you came out here for, like you trying to do something!" I yelled.

The police stopped me before I got too close to him, but I really wished they wouldn't have. He didn't seem like my presence affected him and that made me even madder. I was already feeling some kind of way about Alexus not telling me about the baby shower in the first place. It was like pulling teeth getting her to call or reply to a text, but that was the least she could have done.

I had to find out through one of Eric's girlfriends. She saw it on one of the social media websites and relayed the information to him. I didn't have time to get a gift, so I got a card and put five hundred dollars in it. That was nothing compared to what I wanted to do for the baby, but it was a last-minute option.

"Dude, you just can't stay away, huh?" Tyree said, laughing.

I swear, if the police weren't standing in between us, I would have knocked his ass the fuck out. Two other men came out and stood next to him like that was supposed to scare me. I guess one of them must have been his daddy because they looked so much alike.

"You talking a lot of gangster shit since you got all this backup out here!"

"Backup? Nigga, this ain't no singing group; I don't need no backup. I'm trying to figure out what you want."

"I don't want you." That nigga had jokes but I wasn't in a playing mood.

"There's nothing else here for you."

I looked up and saw Jada standing by the entrance, so I hollered out to her.

"Go call your friend, Jada." She just stood there and looked at me like the dummy she was.

"Nah homie, you don't have anything to say to my wife. Whatever you have to say, you can say it to me," Alexus' man said.

"Your wife! Nigga, you wish that was your wife. Get the fuck outta here!"

"You need to leave. Obviously, you weren't invited," one of the police officers said to me.

His scary ass wasn't saying anything a minute ago, so he could miss me with whatever he was saying now.

"I'm just trying to give my girl her gift and then I'm gone," I noted.

"Your girl?" her boyfriend asked, laughing.

I was about to answer him until I saw Alexus walking outside. She looked good as always, even at eight months pregnant. She walked straight over to him without even acknowledging my presence.

"You could have at least told me that you were having a baby shower. You gon' send his punk ass out here to talk for you, instead of coming to talk for yourself!" I yelled angrily.

"I didn't have to tell you shit. The only person I'm obligated to is my husband," she replied.

I looked over at her ring finger and had to do a double take. She had a huge rock resting on it that wasn't there a few months ago. I couldn't believe it. She was really married. I would usually hear everything that was going on, but this bit of information got by me somehow. That was a slap in the face and a huge blow to my ego. I didn't even think hurt could describe the way I was feeling. I was crushed, but I would never show it.

"It's whatever; I'm just coming to drop off a gift for my baby."

"Your baby?" Alexus replied with her hand on her hip.

"Yeah, my baby until the test says otherwise. I hope you don't have him thinking it's his. I don't give a fuck if that is your husband; no child of mine will be carrying his last name."

"As long as the mama has my last name, I'm cool. Let's go baby," he said arrogantly as he led Alexus away.

"Nigga, you a lame, trying to turn a hoe into a housewife!" I yelled to his departing back.

As mad as I was, I didn't mean what I'd just said. Honestly, if I had the chance, I would have done the exact same thing. With Eric in tow, I walked to my car feeling slightly defeated.

"Damn!" I yelled as I banged my hand against the steering wheel. I'd be lying if I said I didn't feel some kind of way about how things just played out, but it was all good. Alexus and her man had won this battle, but the war was far from being over as far as I was concerned.

Chapter 27

I really hated going to see Dr. Gonzales. Not only was it starting to get uncomfortable for her to check me, but she always seemed to say something that I didn't want to hear. Tyree and I had just left from her office and I was more nervous than ever. In three weeks, I was scheduled to have my baby delivered by cesarean and I was terrified.

Dr. Gonzales didn't think it was a good idea for me to have him naturally because of how big he was. Once she voiced her concerns to my husband, he was on board with whatever the doctor said. I didn't know what to expect and that only intensified my feelings of fear.

Everyone that I asked always told me about the pain that I would experience in the days after I had my baby, and that didn't help at all. Tyree was on the phone telling everybody the good news that I didn't think was good at all. He was so excited. Three weeks was too long of a wait to him, but it wasn't long enough to me.

Thanks to my baby shower, I had everything that I needed for my baby and much more. It took Tyree and his father a whole week to get everything situated and in order. When they took back all the duplicate items, I had over nine hundred dollars put on a gift card. I also had over two thousand dollars in cash and another seven hundred dollars in gift cards as gifts. Tyree decided to take the cash and start a bank account for the baby and that was perfect. The gift cards were put away for anything that he needed later.

Other than Dre showing up and acting a fool, everything about my shower was perfect. He'd been texting me ever since then, telling me that I'd better not give my baby my husband's last name until the test was done. Tyree and I already agreed that we wouldn't name him until the test confirmed who his father was.

Dre already had a son that was a junior, so I didn't know what the big deal was. I told him that the baby could have his last name, but I was deciding on the first name. I couldn't wait until this was all over and done with. If this wasn't Dre's baby, I was changing my number before I even left the hospital. Tyree had already changed his since Kayla and the rest of his exes couldn't comprehend the fact that he was now a married man.

"Do you still want to go to the mall baby?" Tyree asked when he was done talking on the phone.

"No, I'm going with your mama. She wanted to help me pick out some stuff," I replied.

My baby's bag was packed with everything that he needed, but I still needed to get a few things for myself. I wanted a new overnight bag and some more pajamas. Dr. Gonzales said that I would be in the hospital for three days, so I wanted to make sure that I had enough of everything.

"I know you're scared, but everything's going to be alright; I promise," Tyree said lovingly.

"I know it is, but having this baby is not the only thing that scares me. This DNA test is stressing me out too."

"I keep telling you to stop stressing about something that you have no control over. It doesn't matter if Dre is the father, that's still our baby."

"I know," I said lowly.

"Do we need to go over the plan again?" he asked, smiling at me.

"No, I got it. You act like we're on a top secret mission or something."

Tyree and I didn't want any problems when it was time to do the testing at the hospital, so we planned out everything ourselves. We called a DNA testing center that did on the spot testing. They would send one of their nurses out to the hospital to swab the baby, Tyree, Dre, and myself in order to do the test. We paid extra to have the results expedited and the results should be back within twenty-four hours. Jada was responsible for calling Dre to the hospital when it was time for him to be swabbed, but the lab would notify him via phone with the results.

"You want to go home and take a nap before y'all go shopping?"

"I thought you had to go somewhere with your father."

Tyree and his dad were making the house babyproof before the baby arrived. They were putting up safety gates and plug protectors throughout the house, even though I thought it was too soon.

"We are going somewhere, but I can wait until later if you want to go home."

"Well, since I'm hooking up with Tyra anyway, we can head straight over there."

When we arrived at Tyree's parents' house, Jada and the twins decided that they wanted to hang with me and Tyra too. It was still early, so we decided to make a day of it and catch a movie and a bite to eat after our trip to the mall. It was probably going to be my last outing for a while, so I was excited.

After spending almost two hours shopping, I finally had everything that I needed. It wouldn't have taken us so long if we would have stayed out of the baby department. My baby didn't need anything else, but that didn't stop each one of us from buying him something anyway. Jada was going to be the Godmother, so she was really going crazy buying up everything.

"Y'all already know that I'm hungry, so what are we eating?" I asked.

"Damn Lex, we haven't even been out that long," Jada laughed.

"I don't care, I'm starving."

"Seafood it is," Tyra said, already knowing what I wanted.

"Let's go to the crab shack," Jada suggested.

The crab shack was a place that not only sold great seafood, but they also sold bulk seafood to restaurants and the public. Anything that could be made with seafood was made there and I loved it.

"Yes, that sounds like a plan," I cosigned.

We all piled into Tyra's truck and headed to the restaurant. Surprisingly, we were seated as soon as we arrived at the usually overly crowded restaurant. There were a few tables occupied but not as many as usual. We ordered our drinks and appetizers as soon as the waitress came over. Not long after she left, we were interrupted by someone.

"Hey Tyra," we heard coming from behind us. I looked up and saw Kayla and her mother standing near our table.

"Hey Sheila," Tyra said, getting up to give her a hug. Kayla was standing there with that same stupid looking smirk on her face.

"I'm just coming to pick up my order for the restaurant," Sheila volunteered.

"Well, we're coming to feed our faces. My grandbaby loves seafood already," Tyra said, laughing.

"You make sure y'all keep me in mind when one of your events needs catering. I know that baby is going to have a christening or a first birthday party or something that requires food. Y'all know I'll give y'all a good price and I have a huge menu." Sheila sounded like a walking billboard but she knew how to promote her business.

"Ok, I still have the flyers that you sent over last time."

Tyra and Sheila went to school together, so they were longtime friends. While Tyra didn't care too much for Kayla, she genuinely liked her mother.

"I have some new ones with a bigger menu; let me go grab a few from my truck." Shelia was about to walk away when one of the restaurant workers came out with her order.

"I'll come get it from you," Tyra said while following her out.

"Why are you still standing here meat mouth?" Trina sarcastically asked Kayla, as we all laughed.

"Not that it's any of your business, but I'm waiting for my food," she snapped.

"And you need to be worrying about who your baby belongs to, instead of laughing at her corny ass jokes," she said to me.

"Aww, she's a bitter bitch. She almost swallowed a nigga's whole dick and he still changed his number on her. Poor baby," I teased.

"Whatever, bitch; I bet I would have known who my baby's daddy was if I was pregnant."

"Obviously, that don't matter too much because I still got the ring," I said as I waved my hand in the air. "I'm a bad bitch, huh?"

"I don't think so," she replied with her nose turned up in the air.

"Girl, your acting is almost as bad as that weave you're wearing. You're trying hard not to cry right as we speak."

Her food came at the right time because that dam was just about to break. She snatched her bag from the waitress and hauled ass out of the restaurant.

"Well damn, Lex, you really went in on her," Jada laughed.

"Fuck her! She's trying to down me when she's standing there looking like the great pumpkin," I said, referring to the ugly ass orange dress that Kayla had on.

Tyra came walking back inside with a smirk on her face.

"What did y'all tell Kayla? She looked like she wanted to cry when she came outside."

"She wasn't told nothing but the truth," Trina replied. Our waitress came back with our food and we dug right in. After eating so much at the restaurant, we were too full to go to the movies. Knowing me and my condition, I would have gone to sleep anyway. We ended up going back to Tyra's house and watching movies for the rest of the day.

Three weeks later, I was being admitted into the hospital. I couldn't believe how fast that time flew by. My cesarean was schedule for six in the morning. Thanks to my husband and his family, I'd been here since five.

Dr. Gonzales came to check on me, but I barely remembered anything that she said. I was so nervous and I couldn't hide it, even if I wanted to. Only one person was allowed in the operating room so, of course, my husband was coming. It was ten after six, but they still hadn't gotten started. One of the nurses told me that Tyree was washing up and he would be in shortly. I was lying flat on my back, staring at the all-white ceiling. I was hooked up to all kinds of machines, while an IV was pumping medicine into me.

They told me not to be alarmed, but I wouldn't have any feelings in the lower part of my body. When the door opened, I immediately started panicking, thinking that Dr. Gonzales was ready to start. I smiled when I saw that it was Tyree instead.

"What are you wearing?" I laughed. He had on blue scrubs with the matching hat. It almost looked like he was about to be performing the surgery.

"They told me that I had to put this on," he said, laughing with me. He took a seat on the stool that was placed next to my bed.

"I'm scared," I confessed to him for the hundredth time.

"I know, but it'll be over before you know it. I can't wait to see him."

No sooner than the words left his mouth, Dr. Gonzales was walking in.

"How are we doing today, Mr. & Mrs. Taylor?" she asked us.

"We're fine, thanks," Tyree replied.

I didn't say anything, but I watched her every move. She came over and explained the entire process in detail. When she told me that they were ready to get started, I grabbed onto Tyree's hand and held on for dear life. Along with my husband, there was another lady standing next to my bed to make sure I didn't fall asleep. I didn't know why because falling asleep wasn't happening anytime soon. I didn't feel anything, but Tyree kept standing up to see what was happening. Judging by the look on his face, it wasn't a pretty sight.

"Are you alright?" I asked him. He almost looked like he was going to be sick.

"Yeah... yeah, I'm good," he stammered.

"What's going on? What are they doing?"

"I don't even know, but it looks painful. Are you in any pain?"

"Nope, I can't feel a thing." We made small talk for a few more minutes until Dr. Gonzales interrupted us.

"Okay, Mrs. Taylor, you're going to feel a little pressure. That's just us removing the baby. Mr. Taylor, get ready to cut the cord," she said to my husband and me.

Just as she'd said, I felt a little pressure and he was out. Tyree immediately got up and went to cut the cord. I didn't see him, but boy did he have some lungs. He was screaming his little heart out.

"He's a big one," Dr. Gonzales announced. They cleaned him up and wheeled him out of the room.

"I'm going with them; are you going to be alright?" Tyree asked.

"She'll be fine. We need to patch her up and she'll be put into recovery for a little while," Dr. Gonzalez assured him.

Tyree gave me a kiss on the lips before he followed behind the staff and the baby.

After being in recovery for about three hours, I was finally sent to my room. It was already filled with balloons and stuffed animals, courtesy of my family and his. Just like the doctor predicted, my baby weighed a whopping ten pounds, eight ounces. He was so cute and fat, and Tyree couldn't stop holding him.

"He's only a few hours old and you're spoiling him already," Tyra told him.

"You already know that I'm spoiling him rotten."

I kept looking at him, trying to find anything that resembled Dre or Tyree for that matter, but nothing stood out. He had beautiful hair, but that was my doing. It was just too soon for any real features to be visible.

"Hey y'all, the lady from the lab is here," Jada announced when she walked into the room. "She just did Dre, so she needs to do the three of y'all."

The lab tech, who identified herself as Sara, swabbed the baby first; then, she did Tyree and me. We signed the necessary paperwork and it was done. We would be receiving a call around this time tomorrow with the results. We also asked if a copy could be mailed to us, and she agreed. The lab that we chose was expensive, but they had a flawless accuracy rating. I couldn't afford for any mistakes to be made at a time like this.

"Don't worry, we just have to wait and pray," Tyra said to us.

For the remainder of the day, we had many visitors and gifts to come through. It pained me for my baby to simply be referred to as 'baby boy Taylor' instead of a name. That was all my fault for stupid decisions that I made in the past.

"Well, I'm going home; I'll be back tomorrow with the kids," my mother announced after being at the hospital for several hours.

My brother was at her house watching my nieces and nephew, while she spent some time with me. They called me three times already, asking about the baby. They were so excited to have a little cousin and I couldn't wait for them to see him. I hadn't seen Ayanna since I ran into her at my mother's house a few months ago.

"Call me later mama," I said as I gave her a hug.

A few minutes later, Tyra and the rest of Tyree's family were leaving too. It was a little after seven and they'd all been here since five in the morning. I enjoyed their company, but I was happy to be alone with my husband for a while. We had a big day ahead of us tomorrow and both of us would probably be up all night.

"Are you tired?" Tyree asked me.

"Not really. I don't think I'll be going to sleep anytime soon."

"Same here. I'm about to ask the nurse to bring him back in the room."

He took off his shoes and got behind me in the bed and waited for the baby. I guess I must have been more tired than I thought I was because I soon drifted off to sleep.

It was daylight when I woke up the next morning. Tyree was sitting in the recliner flipping through the tv with the baby lying on his chest.

"I thought you said you couldn't sleep," Tyree said, laughing at me.

"I need to go to the bathroom."

"Okay, let me put him down." He stood to his feet and laid the baby down.

After assisting me with my morning hygiene, Tyree left to go grab us some breakfast. I kept looking at the time, wondering when the call from the lab would come in. It was only a little after eight, so we still had about two hours to go. I looked down at my sleeping baby and smiled. Besides me, the other half of his paternity was still a mystery.

"Come in!" I yelled in response to the knock on my door.

One of the nurses came in carrying a huge bouquet of flowers and balloons. It was a beautiful arrangement that instantly put a smile on my face.

"Where should I sit these?" the nurse asked me.

"I'll take it," Tyree said, coming back with our breakfast.

She handed everything over to him before she exited the room. He took the card out of the flowers and handed it over to me. As soon as I opened it and read it, I threw it on the floor and frowned. If I had known that it was from Dre, I would have stopped her before she brought it in.

"What's wrong?" Tyree asked as he sat my food in front of me. He took the baby from me and allowed me to eat.

"It's from Dre," I answered angrily. He picked the card up and sat it on the table.

"Eat your food and stop getting upset over nothing."

Before I had a chance to dig in, my phone started ringing. Tyree grabbed it and passed it over to me.

"It's the lab." My voice quivered and my hands were shaking. They were calling earlier than I expected.

Tyree looked just as nervous as I did but he instructed me to answer the phone. He got up and put the baby in the bed before walking over and sitting down next to me.

"Hello," I answered nervously.

After verifying some information, I listened intently to what the lady on the phone was saying. I closed my eyes as the tears started flowing rapidly. Tyree was begging with his eyes for me to say something, but nothing would come out.

"Thank you," I said before disconnecting the call. I pulled him close to me and held him as tight as I could.

"What did they say?" he asked while drying my tears.

"Congratulations daddy," I said as I smiled at him.

His eyes widened in surprise as he joined me in crying tears of joy. It was confirmed by ninety-nine percent that my husband was the father of our baby boy. Tyree Nassir Taylor III would finally be given his rightful name. We were so overjoyed and I couldn't wait to tell everybody when they came to visit today.

When Tyree finally let me go, he went straight for the baby. He kept kissing him all over his face like he was seeing him for the first time. I grabbed my phone and dialed a number that I'd been waiting to dial forever.

"Who are you calling? I thought you wanted to tell everybody when they got here."

"I'm not calling to tell anybody; I'm calling to get my number changed."

I was sure that Dre got the call confirming the paternity of the baby by now. He was not the father, so he didn't have any reason to contact me ever again. That was the last chapter in the book for us and I was happy that it ended happily for my husband and I.

Chapter 28

I was out with Mya when I got the call from the lab. According to them, there were zero chances that I could have fathered Alexus' baby. I was really hurt because I knew that it was really over between us. I just hated that her new husband was walking away with everything. He already got the girl and, now, he had the baby too.

I always thought that I would be the one to win Alexus' heart in the end, but I was sadly mistaken. I never loved a woman the way I loved her and it hurt to know that she didn't feel the same way. It was cool though because I was done with it all. Another woman would never capture my heart the way that she did and that was a promise that I made to myself. I was doing me from now on, no matter who didn't like it.

I was also done playing games with Cherika. I had my

lawyer to draw up some more divorce papers and she had already been served. I didn't want to go to counseling or anything else that she could think of. I was officially done with being with one woman, including my wife.

She'd been blowing my phone up like crazy, but we didn't have anything to talk about besides the kids. Mya was also trying to secure her a spot, but there was none for her claim. She wasn't the only one that I slept with and she never would be.

Unlike Alexus, Mya didn't mind being the other woman. She was happy to play any position, just as long as she was on the team. She was too clingy and that was what I hated about her the most. Before everything happened with Keanna, she and Mya started getting close. I was happy that it came to an end before it went too far. I didn't need her using my cousin as an excuse to come around all the time. I wanted to be bothered only when I felt like it.

It just so happened that today was her lucky day because we made plans to get a room and chill. I was on my way to bring my kids to their grandmother before I picked her up from work. Cherika sent me a text telling me where to bring them because she wasn't home. Texting was the only way for her to get in contact with me because I never answered her calls.

I pulled up to my soon to be ex mother-in-law's house and helped my kids carry their bags inside. Brenda always spoke to me, but I could tell that I wasn't her favorite person. She thought I did her daughter so wrong, but her daughter wasn't as innocent as she thought she was either. After saying my goodbyes to my babies, I hopped in my truck and headed to go pick up Mya from work.

Chapter 29

I sat on the corner from my mother's house and watched as Dre dropped our kids off. I decided that my mother was right. I wasn't emotionally fit to have my kids right now. I decided to take her up on her offer and let them stay with her for a while. My drinking had gotten out of control and I was starting to take it out on them. I felt like I was losing my mind and I didn't know how to get it back.

It didn't help the situation none when I was once again served with divorce papers a few days ago. Dre listed the reason as irreconcilable differences. Nothing about infidelity was ever mentioned, but that was the only problem that we had. I tried calling him to talk, but he never answered my calls. He only answered my text messages if I was talking about the kids.

Then, to make matters worse, he had about a million other women that he was texting and dealing with. Since all his texts were still coming to my iPad, I knew what he was doing every time he did it. None of them bothered me as much as the last text that he sent to Eric, talking about Alexus. He was pissed about her changing her phone number and he vented to his brother about it. Apparently, she had gotten married and he was feeling some kind of way about it. Then, to my delight, he found out that her baby wasn't his. He went on to say how he had never loved anyone else the way that he loved her and he never would.

Being that I'm his wife, that was a huge slap in my face. It was also the last straw. I was tired of being Dre's doormat and letting him walk all over me. Thanks to the text messages, I saw that he was hooking up with Mya tonight and that was perfect. I wanted to confront both of them at the same time. I watched and waited until my kids were safely inside before I started following Dre. I didn't know where he was going and I really didn't care. I had a tank full of gas and nothing but time on my hands.

I made sure that I stayed at least two to three cars behind him, but I never let him out of my sight. When he hopped on the bridge, I was right there behind him. After a while, I figured out where we were going. He pulled into the parking lot of the rehabilitation center where he once lived, and Mya came running out. She got into the front seat and gave him a peck on the lips before he pulled off. Any doubts I had were permanently removed the moment their lips touched. I wiped the tears from my eyes as I continued my pursuit. They didn't know it yet, but their fun was about to be cut short at any moment.

Chapter 30

"**D**amn!" I yelled as I frantically searched the truck for my wallet. I pulled to the side of the road and checked under my seat and in the back to see if had fallen from my pocket.

"What's wrong?" Mya asked.

"I think I left my wallet at home."

I didn't remember if I left it at home or if it fell out of my pocket. The only place I went was to drop my kids off at their grandmother's house, so it couldn't have been far. I called Brenda and asked her to check outside of her house, but she didn't see it either. I couldn't drive all the way across town without my wallet, but I didn't want Mya coming with me to my house either. But, then again, she lived too far away to bring her home and then go back to my house.

"Well, go home and get it. It's not a big deal," she replied, unconcerned.

Her ass must have really thought I was stupid. She'd been trying to get to my house for a few months, but it'd never happened. But, from the looks of it, that was about to change.

"I really don't have a choice," I said as I headed in the direction of my house.

I looked at her from the corner of my eye. She smiled slightly, but I was about to wipe it right off of her face. She was coming to my house, but she damn sure wasn't coming inside.

When I pulled up to the gate, I saw that it was open, but the guard wasn't in his booth. I drove right through and headed towards the back to my condo.

"It's nice back here." Mya looked around the subdivision and nodded in approval.

I ignored her and kept driving until I pulled up in front of my place.

"Can I come in and use the bathroom?" Mya slyly asked.

"Hell no! You just left from your office. You should have used the bathroom there!"

"Please Dre, I can't hold it any longer."

"You can either squat on the side of this truck or wait until we get to the room." My reply was harsh but she was starting to piss me off by trying to be slick.

"I can't believe that you're acting like this. It's only going to take me a minute to use the bathroom while you get your wallet."

"Come on, with your sneaky ass. And don't go in there looking all around and touching shit. Use the bathroom and come out," I said as I got out of the truck.

"Okay," she said excitedly as she got out on the passenger's side. As soon as I opened the door, she flew right past me and into the house.

"It's so pretty in here. Alexus must really have some good taste. I know you didn't decorate like this." She was looking around like she was picturing herself living here.

"Go use the bathroom and let's go."

I pointed to the bathroom door to show her where it was. I just told her stupid ass not to come in here looking around and that's the first thing that she did.

"Okay, I'm going." She disappeared down the hall.

I went into my room and was happy when I saw my wallet sitting on my dresser. I grabbed it and stuffed it in my back pocket and turned to leave. I jumped when I turned around and saw Mya standing in the doorway.

"I thought you had to use the bathroom?"

"I did; I used it already."

"Stop lying, you didn't use the bathroom that damn fast."

"Why are you always paying for a hotel room when you have this nice house? We can spend some nights over here sometimes," Mya said, walking into the room and sitting on the bed.

"Let's go Mya, don't even try to get comfortable."

"Can't we just chill here for a little while?" she asked while pissing me off at the same time.

"No! Hell no! I told you that I don't bring women anywhere where my kids lay their heads."

"But you brought Alexus here to live with you. You said so yourself."

She was really starting to get under my skin with bringing Alexus up every five minutes. She was starting to

233

remind me of Cherika and it was turning me off. I was already having second thoughts about spending the night with her.

"Don't worry about what I did with Alexus. This was our house together and that was my girl."

"So, what am I to you?" she asked, looking hopeful.

"Yeah Dre, what is she to you?"

I really thought I was losing my mind when I turned around and saw Cherika standing in the doorway.

"How the hell did you get in here? As a matter of fact, what are you doing here at all?" I asked her.

"So, you couldn't bring me to your house, but your side bitches are welcomed with opened arms," she said, referring to Mya.

"I got your bitch," Mya replied.

"Mya, shut up. Cherika, you need to leave," I said calmly.

"Yeah Cherika, you need to go," Mya repeated.

"Mya!" I yelled, looking at her with fire in my eyes. I didn't need her to talk for me and I didn't ask her to.

"So, if you never loved anyone the way you loved Alexus, how did you feel about me, your wife?" Cherika asked.

"What the hell are you talking about?"

She threw her iPad, which I never even noticed in her hand, on the floor at my feet. I just looked at it, then back up at her in confusion.

"Pick it up and read," she instructed.

"Man, I'm not picking that shit up."

She reached behind her back and pulled out a gun, aiming it right at me. Mya gasped and covered her mouth, as my heart sank to my feet. I always told her that she was crazy, but the look in her eyes right now proved that theory.

"Pick it up and read," she repeated calmly.

I bent down and picked up the iPad. The screen was black, so I pressed the round button at the bottom to turn it on. After sliding the bar over, I read what appeared on the screen. My mouth dropped as I read over every text message that I sent or received over the past few months. Now, I knew what she was talking about. She saw the texts between me and Eric. I was expressing my feelings to him about Alexus. I was hurt about the baby not being mine, but I was even more hurt about her being married. Cherika was never supposed to see that but, unfortunately, she did.

"It's not even like that Cherika," I replied hesitantly.

"Just shut up Dre because everything that comes out of your mouth is a lie. You never had any intentions on working things out with me. You are never going to change and I'm tired of fighting." She tried her best to talk through the tears.

"Cherika, you know things haven't been right with us for a long time. We just need some time apart and maybe we can try again when-"

"Shut up!" she yelled, cutting me off. "I'm so tired of you lying to me all the time. You keep telling me what I want to hear, but you don't mean what you say. Things haven't been right with us because you can't keep your dick in your pants. Then, you send me divorce papers like I'm the problem when all along it's been you. I've come to realize that no matter what I do, I'll never be good enough for you. You'll never be satisfied with just me. I'd rather see you dead than with bitches like her," she said, pointing to Mya.

"Dre had you right. You really are crazy. You can't force a man to be with you," Mya said angrily.

"Mya, shut the fuck up!" I yelled in amazement. I couldn't believe her stupid ass had a gun pointed right at her and was still talking shit. I knew for sure that, if I made it out of this alive, I was through with her.

"Yeah Mya, shut the fuck up," Cherika said as she turned the gun on her and pulled the trigger.

I jumped at the loud sound, as Mya fell backwards on the bed. The small hole in her chest immediately started pouring blood.

"Oh shit!" I yelled as I ran over to her. Her eyes were open, but she sounded like she was gasping for air.

"Get away from her!" Cherika yelled at me.

I was shocked at what I was seeing. I never imagined that Cherika would do something like this. Her mind was somewhere else because it definitely wasn't here.

"Cherika, don't do this. The girl is dying; let me get her some help," I begged through teary eyes.

"Let her die; get away from her!"

I couldn't move as I looked at Mya fighting hard to breathe. When I heard the gurgling sounds coming from her mouth, I knew that her battle was in vain. I put my hand over hers and watched helplessly as she took her last breath. I looked up at Cherika and the satisfied look on her face disgusted me.

"Is it that serious Cherika? Is being married to me serious enough for you to take her life?" I asked her with hate filled eyes.

"Till death do us part, right?" she countered as she pointed the gun at me.

I raised my hands in the air and tried my best to reason with her.

"So, you're really going to take me away from my kids?" I was trying my best to gain some sympathy.

"You don't care about them. You don't care about anybody but you, and you always have. Loving you is literally killing me, but why should I be the only one to die," she said with a crazed look in her eyes.

Before thinking about it any further, I lunged toward her in an attempt to pull the gun away from her. I was stopped in my tracks when she pulled the trigger and the hot lead entered my mid-section. I dropped to the floor, as the pain seemed to travel throughout my entire body. I'd never been shot before, but death had to be better than the pain that I was experiencing. I lived in a quiet upscale community, so I prayed that somebody heard the gun shots and came to intervene.

"Since we couldn't be together in life, maybe we can be together in death." Cherika was muttering more to herself than to me.

I turned on my stomach and tried to crawl away but was stopped by another shot to my back. My body jerked when the hot lead entered it. I felt the sharp pain and the heat from the bullet but, after a few seconds, the pain went away and I felt numb. I thought I was having a panic attack because my breaths were coming short and quick. Reaching for my phone wasn't an option because I couldn't move. I was losing my battle with consciousness, but I put up a good fight.

I heard Cherika mumbling something, but I couldn't make out what she was saying. I didn't want to believe that my actions drove her to this, but I knew that they did. I played with her feelings so many times without thinking about the end result. As many times as Cherika threatened to take my life, I never really took her seriously. It always seemed to be said out of anger. I just figured that once she calmed down, everything would be alright, but not this time. R. Kelly was absolutely right. When a woman's fed up, it ain't nothing you can do about it.

"God, please forgive me and protect my babies," was the last thing I heard before a single gunshot went off.

A single tear rolled from my eye at the thought of my wife and the mother of my kids taking her own life because of me.

Chapter 31

Alexus and I were just leaving the clinic from bringing Tre to his two-week checkup. I couldn't see it at first but, as the days turned into weeks, my son was starting to look just like me. He had thick black hair just like his mother, but everything else he got from me. He was fat as hell and I was having fun spoiling him already. I couldn't keep my mama and daddy away from the house since he came home from the hospital. I didn't mind because I needed all the help I could get. Alexus was in a lot of pain for the first few days, so she really couldn't help out too much. Thankfully, she was feeling much better and I was happy for that.

"Where do you want to go now?" I asked my wife.

"It doesn't matter; I'm just happy to be outside."

Alexus' doctor didn't think she should be outside for at least four to six weeks. Needless to say, I was doing whatever Dr. Gonzales said. Since she seemed to be going crazy from being inside for so long, I agreed to let her stay out today after our son's doctor's appointment.

"We can go get something to eat or we can go visit your mama and the kids.

"Okay, that's cool."

We drove around and talked about where we wanted to eat. I was just proceeding through a green light, preparing to get on the bridge when Alexus started screaming.

"Baby, stop!" she yelled, scaring the hell out of me.

"What's wrong? What am I stopping for?"

"Turn around and go back under the bridge," she instructed frantically.

"What am I turning around for?" I did what I was told but I still wanted to know what was up.

"Just go back, please."

After making a U-turn, I pulled up under the bridge like she asked me to. They had people on mattresses and lounge chairs as if they were at home. Of course, all eyes were on us when we pulled up to the crowd in a silver Jaguar. Alexus was about to get of the car, but I stopped her before she could.

"Where the hell are you going?" I asked while pulling her by her arm.

"Right there, look," she said as she pointed to someone.

"Who the hell is that?"

"That's my sister," she replied as she got out of the car.

My mouth flew open in shock as I watched my wife walk up to Ayanna. If she would have passed me on the streets, I would have never recognized her. She looked like she weighed no more than one hundred pounds on a good day. Her skin was ashy and her hair was barely there. The white shirt that she wore was dingy and full of stains. The jogging pants were rolled up at least three times, just to stay up around her thin waist. Her arms were full of track marks where she pushed the needle in her veins. Worst of all was the hollow area in her mouth where her front teeth used to be. I watched for a while as my wife talked to her about I didn't know what, but I got concerned when they started walking towards the car. When Ayanna got closer, the sight was even worse than I thought. Alexus opened the back door and allowed her sister to peek in at the baby, and the smell that entered my nostrils was anything but pleasant.

"I can't believe that I got a nephew," Ayanna said in her raspy voice. "He's so cute."

I was both relieved and happy when Alexus finally closed the door. It's sad to say, but there was no way in hell that she was holding my baby and I didn't care how my wife felt about it. I continued waiting patiently while they stood outside the car and talked. After a few minutes, Alexus opened the door and grabbed her purse.

"What are you doing?" I asked.

"I'm just giving her a few dollars, so she can get a few things that she needs."

"No, the hell you're not!" I yelled as I snatched her purse away from her.

"Tyree please, she just needs to get some more clothes and underwear."

"Alexus, no, look at her. Do you really think she's going to buy anything besides drugs if you give her money?"

A man, who I assumed was her boyfriend, walked over and put his arms around her tiny waist. He looked just as bad as she did, if not worse.

"What's up Lex?" he spoke to my wife.

"Don't speak to me, Troy," Lex snapped.

By now, I was out of the car and standing at my wife's side. One thing I knew for sure and that was never to trust a drug addict.

"Do you have that for me, Lex?" Ayanna asked, trying to whisper.

"Nah, we don't have no money," I said loud enough for both of them to hear.

"Y'all riding around in an eighty-thousand-dollar car, but y'all don't have any money?" Ayanna's man said.

"Nigga, don't worry about what the fuck we ride around in. My wife is not supporting nobody's drug habit," I said, going off.

"Who said anything about drugs?" Ayanna questioned defensively.

"Girl, you sound stupid. You look like you've been having those clothes on for a week. Obviously, you haven't been too worried about changing clothes. Why are you so worried about now?"

"Lex, please," she said, begging my wife.

"I can't Ayanna," Lex replied sadly.

"Let's go baby, fuck them," her man said, leading her away from us.

They were barely three steps away from us before Alexus broke down crying. I wrapped my arms around her and held her tight. I felt so bad for her, but I really didn't know what to say.

"Come on baby." I helped her get into the car before I got in.

"She looks so bad." She cried her heart out as I drove away from her sister.

"I know, baby, but there's really nothing that you can do for her. Giving her money is hurting her more than it's helping. Now, if you want to make sure that she eats or takes a bath or whatever, I'll be happy to help you do that."

"Yes, I definitely want to do that," she said, perking up a little.

"Okay, we'll stay in touch and make sure she's good."

"Thank you, baby; I really appreciate that," she said as she leaned over and gave me a kiss.

She wiped her face and smiled at me and that was good enough. I couldn't stop her sister from using drugs and neither could she, but as long as my wife was happy, then so was I.

Chapter 32

It'd been a little over three months since I'd been locked up and I'd already gotten into three fights. I was the new girl, so I was constantly tested. The vicious scars on my face didn't help me all that much with making friends. The police eventually caught up with Lee, but he still hadn't been sentenced for what he did to me yet. The DA told me that he was a repeat offender so, hopefully, he wouldn't be getting out anytime soon.

Thankfully, my uncle EJ got me a lawyer, but he still wasn't much help. I was charged with second degree feticide, two counts of battery, and trespassing. The battery count was increased because Malik and his girlfriend had also called the police on me after I used my Taser on him. They also slapped a trespassing charge on me for going to their house uninvited.

I was facing twenty-five years unless I took the plea

deal that was being offered by the prosecutor. Under the plea deal, I would get ten years and be eligible for parole in eight. My uncle EJ didn't want me to take a chance in court because he knew that I would lose. The evidence was too strong for me to win. The young guy that worked in the store was more than willing to testify and I just couldn't take that chance.

So, before I was scheduled to go to trial, I informed my lawyer that I wanted to plead guilty and accept the offer that was given to me. That was a decision that I regret to this day. Not long after that, Cherika was facing some charges of her own. Apparently, she snapped and was now facing first degree and attempted first degree murder charges.

According to what my uncle EJ said, she followed Dre and Mya to Dre's house and shot both of them before turning the gun on herself. Miraculously, Cherika survived a self-inflicted gunshot to the head, but Mya wasn't as fortunate. She died from a single gunshot to her chest.

Unfortunately, Dre would be confined to a wheelchair for the rest of his life, after being on the receiving end of his wife's gun. He could have healed from the wound to his stomach, but the shot to his lower back affected his central nervous system and caused permanent paralysis. He was now living with my uncle EJ because he couldn't do much of anything on his own. My uncle said that Cherika's mom had the kids, but they visited their father every weekend.

I felt so guilty about so many things because I knew that I was the cause of a lot of it. I started a chain of unfortunate events the moment I introduced Dre and Alexus. I started out trying to get back at Cherika for sleeping with Troy, but things quickly got out of hand from there. My jealously and hatred for Alexus had me blind.

Even now as I sat in this dingy cell, she constantly ran across my mind. I did so much to bring her down, but she always managed to come out on top. She had the life that many women could only dream of. She was smart and she proved that by getting her degree. She had a damn good husband and now they had a son. Maybe if I would have put more energy into doing the right thing, I wouldn't be in the position I was in now. It was too late to cry about the past. My fate was sealed for the next eight to ten years and there was nothing that I could do to change it. One thing was for sure; I had a lot of time to sit and reflect on all the mistakes that I made in the past and that was exactly what I planned to do.

PROLOGUE

(3 years later)

I sat on the front row of the church, along with my mother, siblings, nieces and nephew, staring straight ahead as the pastor spoke. My husband held my hand tightly, in hopes of giving me comfort.

Tre, now three years old, sat one row back with his grandparents, while our five-month-old daughter, Tyriel, sat on Tyree's lap. I looked back and smiled at Jada and the twins who were seated a few rows behind us. The church wasn't overly crowded, but every pew was filled with a mixture of family and friends. The huge picture that sat at the head of the casket was the only way to tell who the deceased woman was. I looked at it carefully and tried hard to remember how my sister was before the drugs took over her life and eventually killed her. It was so hard to remember the good times since we never really had many to begin with.

True to his word, Tyree made sure that I saw Ayanna at least twice a week. He was skeptical about bringing her to our house, but he would always let her take a shower in one of his vacant properties. I always made sure that she had a clean change of clothes and a hot meal before we dropped her back off to wherever she wanted to go.

After doing this for a few months, Ayanna up and disappeared on us. We would pass through the areas that she was known to hang around, but she was never there. Either no one had seen her or we would have just missed her right before we came. Then, out of nowhere, she would show up to one of her old hangouts and we would start the process all over again.

I thought that she had pulled a disappearing act on us again this last time, but that wasn't the case. Instead of going to pick her up and giving her a hot meal, I was going to the morgue to identify her body. She was found in an abandoned house, dead from a drug overdose.

I was heartbroken, but not more than my mother was. She predicted Ayanna's death at the hands of the streets a long time ago. It pained her to have to make arrangements to bury one of her children, so my husband and I had to do it for her. I couldn't imagine how my nieces and nephews felt, especially since they hadn't seen their mother in over a year. They didn't cry, so there was no way to gauge their reaction.

I watched silently as the visitors walked up to Ayanna's casket for the final viewing. A lone tear escaped my eye as a nurse in pink colored scrubs wheeled a weeping man to the front of the church to view. He was only about thirty years old, but the sickness that ate away at his body made him look twice as old.

Troy had been diagnosed with full blown aids about a year before Ayanna died. He was still an active drug user, so his condition declined rapidly. When he was admitted into a nursing home about six months ago, Ayanna started running with another group of junkies and things only got worse. As much as I wanted to hate him, something inside of me couldn't do it. I had to come to terms with my sister's drug use without putting the blame on anyone else. We all had choices and she made the wrong ones.

I thought back to some of the choices I'd made and I silently thanked God for bringing me out alive. After years of sleeping with another woman's husband, that could have easily been me lying cold in a coffin for the entire world to see. Cherika had finally snapped and another woman was dead because of it. Dre was confined to a wheelchair and, after trying to take her own life, Cherika was doing time in a crazy house. She pled temporary insanity and avoided going to jail. The newspapers called it a crime of passion and she gained a lot of sympathy from the public.

I still spoke with her mother from time to time, but I hadn't seen her in a while. She was raising the kids, along with the help of Dre and his family. Brenda was still a praying woman and I knew that prayer was the only thing that got her through it all.

After viewing my sister's remains, we all headed to my mother's house for a small repast. Ayanna's remains were being cremated, so we didn't have to go to a burial site. After fixing Tre and my husband something to eat, I excused myself and went to the ladies' room. Feeling blessed, I didn't waste any time dropping down to my knees and giving God thanks for bringing me this far. I had so many things to be thankful for and I didn't take any of it for granted.

I have a great career, a loving husband and two beautiful kids. I may have gone through the fire, but I came out as pure gold.

Made in the USA
Coppell, TX
18 November 2021

66001699R00138